THE
DISCOVERY
OF
LIGHT

Also by J. P. Smith

The Blue Hour
Body and Soul
The Man from Marseille

THE
DISCOVERY
OF
LIGHT

J. P. SMITH

VIKING

VIKING
Published by the Penguin Group
Viking Penguin, a division of Penguin Books USA Inc.,
375 Hudson Street, New York, New York 10014, U.S.A.
Penguin Books Ltd, 27 Wrights Lane, London W8 5TZ, England
Penguin Books Australia Ltd, Ringwood, Victoria, Australia
Penguin Books Canada Ltd, 10 Alcorn Avenue, Suite 300,
Toronto, Ontario, Canada M4V 3B2
Penguin Books (N.Z.) Ltd, 182–190 Wairau Road,
Auckland 10, New Zealand

Penguin Books Ltd, Registered Offices: Harmondsworth, Middlesex, England

First published in 1992 by Viking Penguin,
a division of Penguin Books USA Inc.

1 3 5 7 9 10 8 6 4 2

PUBLISHER'S NOTE
This is a work of fiction. Names, characters, places, and incidents
either are the product of the
author's imagination or are used
fictitiously, and any resemblance to actual persons, living or
dead, events, or locales is entirely coincidental.

LIBRARY OF CONGRESS CATALOGING IN PUBLICATION DATA
Smith, J. P., 1949–
The discovery of light/ J. P. Smith.
p.   cm.
ISBN 0–670–83903–5
I. Title.
PS3569.M53744D5   1992
813'.54—dc20   91–16754

Printed in the United States of America
Set in Perpetua
Designed by Brian Mulligan

for René Belletto

Pour Ver Meer de Delft, elle lui de-
manda s'il avait souffert par une
femme, si c'était une femme qui l'avait
inspiré . . .

—Proust, *A la Recherche du temps perdu*

He would be in the painting himself, in his bedroom, almost at the top on the right, like an attentive little spider weaving his shimmering web, standing, beside his painting, with his palette in his hand, with his long grey smock all stained with paint, and his violet scarf.

—Georges Perec, *La Vie mode d'emploi*

With grateful thanks to the faculty and facilities of the Montserrat College of Art in Beverly, Massachusetts; and especially to Professor Roger H. Martin, whose booming voice and learned advice more than once put me back in the picture.

THE
DISCOVERY
OF
LIGHT

THE DISCOVERY
OF LIGHT

It can only be late afternoon.

The light coming through the window is a wan autumnal haze on the wall, and yet the woman holding the balance, the woman who weighs pearls and gold, seems softly radiant as the frail beam breaks upon her, as if there were something hallowed about this captured moment.

Winter is coming. We know it from the jacket the woman wears, the ermine trim that keeps her warm. Yet it's impossible for us to spy an outer world: men driving carts through cobblestone streets, women sweeping the dust from their thresholds, children bundled in woolens, playing at hoops along the canal. We know it's there, though, we see the glow from the sky, but we sense that things are quiet. Perhaps snow is expected. People sit by their fires, waiting for the flakes to fall from the grey unbroken overcast.

It doesn't matter. Clearly the artist means us to contemplate the stillness and consequence of the event in the room. The woman is holding the empty scales between the thumb and forefinger of her right hand, testing their accuracy, and suddenly, at this late hour, after a long day's weighing, they achieve perfect equilibrium.

She has seen this happen many times; and each time, perhaps, she has found a certain pleasure in it. Perhaps, too, this is to be the last task of her day. It's difficult to say.

For hers is a face that is impossible to look into, her expression indecipherable. The woman is oblivious to you. She is busy but unrushed, she has pearls and gold to weigh: a precise but effortless trade, one that demands time and patience, a good eye, a steady hand. The balance she holds seems to be reflected in her poise, her cool intelligent smile, the gentle pressure of the fingers of her left hand on the table. There is also the suggestion that another mystery has yet to be solved: that swelling which separates the two panels of her jacket: boy or girl?

Behind her, in a painting on the wall, terror and salvation as, sword in hand, the Son of God weighs souls. Sinners tumble headlong into hell; the elect sit on the cloud with their Judge: no one will escape this terrible day. So the woman weighing is surrounded by emblems of heaven and earth, she is a fulcrum in the middle of a simile. Yet the woman is in a world of her own, somehow removed from the simple lesson represented here; suspended between the life that grows within her and the fate illustrated in the painting on the wall; detached from things, remote from you, held forever in the amber of uncertainty.

As in a still life we sense that the carefully arranged grapes and pears and apples have reached their moment of ripeness, that in another hour or two decay will set in, we feel that what has been caught in this room, in this painting, this exquisite moment of repose and precision, of commencement and conclusion, will dissolve into a kind of chaos. The artist seems to be saying: this is the way things are arranged, in life and at the moment of our death, and this woman who weighs the objects of this world, the gold and pearls, not even she will escape what we know to be inevitable. Everything can be measured.

Yet she fears nothing. She is serene. She accepts things for what they are. She is merely an image on a canvas and so can feel neither joy nor sorrow, hope or despair. The day is drawing to a close in this liquid world of Delft, and there are no true certainties, neither in this place, nor in any other.

SMOKE

Very still.

That's how I recall her. Motionless.

In some obscure way the woman in the painting, the woman weighing pearls and gold, had always reminded me of Kate: her mouth, her eyes, her otherness, the mystery of her. The impossibility of putting her into words. The way she seems to shimmer between precision and ambiguity. I could go on and on.

Kate also enjoyed being something of an enigma, it kept her two steps apart from me, gave her that much more breathing space. "What are you thinking?" I would sometimes ask her, and she would look at the painting of the woman with the scales and, lowering her eyes, smile.

I was in London to promote my third novel, which contrary to my publisher's expectations had been a critical success in the States. Kate was then an editor at a prestigious British publishing house based in a quiet Bloomsbury square. I had just moved to Massachusetts and a teaching job after a divorce from a musician whose marriage to me, if it could be called that, had lasted barely over a year. We were two self-involved artists, enveloped in our separate worlds, spiteful, envious, circling furtively around each other's careers in our SoHo loft, miserable in that city of glass. It had taken a great deal out of us, it had broken our spirits, this discord and strife, this venom. I'd always wondered why we'd bothered to go through with it in the first place. We rarely saw each other. On most days she was uptown teaching classes; in the evenings performing with a trio, a quartet, a jug band: whoever would pay her. I was at home, typing, listening to music, gazing out the window. Occasionally I would spend my afternoons browsing in record shops, killing time, walking the familiar district where madmen ranted on street corners and steam oozed from the gutters.

Kate and I met for lunch at a restaurant near her office two days after my arrival. There was no great hurry: the book had been edited in New York and her firm had merely paid for the rights to reprint it. There was nothing for her to do but ensure the novel was sent out for reviews, arrange for publicity. Until then she had been a signature on a letter, a voice on my hotel room phone: quiet, scarcely above a whisper; as tantalizing as ectoplasm.

"I'm awfully busy this week," she said. "But I think I can fit you in on Wednesday."

I knew no one in London save for the Indian gentleman in charge of the hotel desk, a Mr. Mistry, who recommended cheap eateries and interesting nightclubs, and who, whenever I walked into the lobby with a bag of fast food or Chinese take-away, shook his finger at me and said, "Mr. Reid, you are young, you must eat properly." But I was uncomfortable dining alone in public. It reminded me of old age, of the displaced people who sometimes drift in solitude through the pages of my novels, moving from café terrace to restaurant, living on their memories, harboring secrets, haunting me with their shadowy presence, their parchment skin;

like comets, trailing behind them the dust of their journeys. I would watch them from the window of my grandmother's New York apartment when I was a child, ancient men with their newspapers and umbrellas on a breezy day in Washington Heights.

We met at her office and walked to a pub near the British Museum. I was due to return to the States a week later. I planned on seeing some plays, touring museums when I wasn't being interviewed or promoting my book. I hadn't been to London in years. I considered flying to Paris for a few days. I was happy for the company and I wanted this meal to last for hours.

She said: "I lived in France for three years. Actually I was back there last spring. Paris was lovely."

"I've never been."

"You must go. I envy you. The first time is always the best."

"Do you really enjoy doing this, taking your authors out for their token lunch?"

"No. Not really."

"What would you prefer to be doing?"

"Translating other people's books. That's why I took this job. To make some contacts, meet people. Nobody sane wants to be an editor forever."

"I like your accent."

"I've done some work already, just short pieces, an article or two."

"It's very attractive. Your accent, I mean." I sipped my drink. "Seductive. Very nice."

"Of course I'd prefer to be translating books. I'm going to continue to ignore your comments, by the way."

She was as cool as the ice in my Scotch. "I've decided I'm going to Paris after all," I said.

"Bon voyage."

"But you see you've talked me into it."

She took a typed page from her bag and passed it across the

table to me. "We've set up two appointments for you tomorrow. You're to be interviewed for an arts review program on Radio 4 to be taped in the morning at eleven, and another with the *Guardian* for the afternoon. There's no guarantee either will be used, but it's worth giving it a go. I'll ring you at the hotel afterwards just to see how they went and to let you know what we've got lined up for Friday. Here are the addresses. I don't think there's any need for me to accompany you."

"I'll be lost, you know."

"At the BBC?"

"In Paris."

"Ask the gendarmes for directions."

"I don't speak French."

"Buy a map, for God's sake."

Kate had shoulder-length blond hair which made my heart melt. Her smile was candid, unmistakably genuine. She was like someone you see in a movie or a spread in a fashion magazine, aloof yet astonishingly present; invariably beyond your reach. She was a pane of glass, I the boy with a stone: the temptation to throw hung between us like a dare. And when I asked when she'd like to go with me to Paris, tomorrow or maybe the day after, or possibly she preferred to toss caution to the wind and leave in ten minutes, she laughed and shook her head and then stopped laughing and looked at me, directly at my eyes, and I think I knew then that I would never let her go. She said: "I liked your book very much. No, really I did. Did I say that already?"

"Say it again."

"I liked it a lot."

"A great deal?"

She smiled.

"You couldn't put it down?"

"No."

"Really?"

"Really," she said, laughing again.

"Was it the best thing you'd read all year?"

"One of the best."

"Was it brilliant?"

"In its own perverse way," she said, her eyes sparkling with amusement.

"A masterpiece?"

"If you like."

"Then you're going with me to Paris." My divorce had given me the urge to take risks, speak my mind, seek the exhilaration of danger, toy with failure.

She looked at me for what seemed a long time. I sipped my drink. I had nothing to lose. She said: "All right."

"But you don't even know me."

"First you talk me into going with you to Paris, now you're making excuses. Like Kafka," and she laughed.

And I said: "I just want to make sure you know what you're getting into."

Kate said, "I've read your books. Of course they have a certain reputation."

"They're not me."

"I know. I know. They always say that."

"So who is it, really, you'll be going to Paris with?"

She smiled again. "I'll find out soon enough." And I remember that smile as she crossed the border into my life.

Just as I remember the evening she left me, two years and three thousand miles later.

There was a sense of calm, of two reasonable people coming to an agreement, drawing away from each other, drowning in the silent air of a late September afternoon. Beyond that only details: a spider in the bath, a red stain on the rug, a cloud passing over the moon, distant laughter; insignificant things that remained outside our drama and in my memory sometimes threatened to absorb a certain weight, become emblematic. A cloud, a stain, a spider; laughter. Images that shrouded a deeper violence.

Perhaps because there had been so little emotion attached to our separation it seemed as if Kate had simply gone off to visit relatives in New York; in fact she had traveled there to spend a week or two at her sister's. It was to be a temporary separation: she said she needed time to consider things, to regain her equilibrium.

Often that last year she had seemed distant from me, as if her attention were elsewhere, beyond the walls of the room. Conversation would be reduced to fragments of sentences, isolated words, yeses and nos and maybes. She seemed somehow to lose definition, as though she were going out of focus, becoming a blur amidst the planes and angles of our house near the lake. And then for four or five days she would seem to slip away from our marriage, from me, from herself; a stranger, standing apart, watching the two of us with incomprehension and a kind of horror, as though at such moments she possessed some special insight, a vision that went beyond the laughter and tenderness and companionship to reveal something terrifying: decay, dissolution, things of a dark nature.

A cloud, a stain, a spider; laughter.

I remember the morning she died.

It was just past nine when the phone rang. Josie said: "Did I wake you?" and I knew something had happened, I sensed it in the tone of her voice, the way her crisp English accent crumbled like a broken biscuit.

Kate had somehow stumbled while waiting for a train. Her sister said, "She must have lost her footing. The police phoned us a few minutes ago."

She had died an hour earlier. Josie called it *passing on*.

"She said she wanted to go back."

I listened.

"Everything seemed all right the night before."

Yes?

"She left before we woke."

She was standing on the subway platform, waiting for a train. To take her where? The airport? To Grand Central to connect with a shuttle bus? Yet she hadn't called to tell me she was coming home, I knew nothing about it.

She had thought things over, she was returning to me.

Or she had thought things over and she was about to leave me for good. Now I would never know. I could see her descending the stairs of the station, in a moment of clarity I could hear the train approaching, I could see Kate walking the length of the platform, and then seeming to catch her attention I blinked and she disappeared.

This was no accident.

Josie said, "David?"

I replaced the receiver and tried to catch my breath, I pressed my hands to my face, I hid my eyes and felt my head spin, the world reeling around me as though my center of gravity had fallen away, or shifted, and could no longer be located.

I tried to imagine what had happened that morning, in the moments just before it occurred, tried to find some correlation between my sensations, my intuition, and the death of my wife. For some reason I thought of her becoming completely calm, as one does just after waking, after the rapture and turmoil of dreams, the body slowly and serenely adjusting to the contours of a more solid world. I awoke at eight and by nine was at my desk, over which hung a reproduction of a painting by Vermeer, a woman weighing gold and pearls.

I felt compelled to see the whole of her life, to trace its curve with a fingertip, enclose it within myself as if it were an object that wholly belonged to me, something precious. I strove for structure and completion, as though our life together were something lying in my desk drawer, sixty thousand dispassionate words neatly typed on clean white paper.

She must have lost her footing.

She had stepped in front of a train, yet instead she could have taken an overdose of tranquilizers, become drowsy, fallen into endless sleep. But of course she hated taking pills. Possibly she had contemplated drowning herself. Yet she was a strong swimmer, and I can see her in her black bathing suit, standing on the beach, smiling, alive, her hand raised to shade her eyes from the bright sunlight. Had she walked into the water she would have fought to save herself; instinct would have taken over.

I thought of her alone, at the edge of the platform, hearing the train approaching, feeling the ground tremble, coming to a sudden decision. It seemed a nineteenth-century decision, inevitable, something out of a novel.

Lost her footing, passing on: as though Kate had stepped into a world of euphemism and code.

Small practicalities came to mind. I would have to speak of Kate's death to others: friends, relatives, the remnants of her family. What she had done had happened in a moment outside of time, beyond words.

She had always wished to be cremated. That night of our separation was the last I had seen of her. The accident had left her body shattered, her face broken. It was pointless to reconstruct her. She was an unadorned pine box moving slowly and silently away from me. Two doors flapped open and through my tears I saw the flames take her.

The director of the crematorium handed me Kate's possessions, tidily wrapped in a brown paper parcel: her coat and shoes and wedding ring. Her suitcase and bag, which she'd probably left on the edge of the subway platform, had disappeared, been taken by someone drawn to the scene, to the imagined riches she had left behind. In her coat pocket was a torn movie ticket and a postcard she had bought at the Frick Collection, a painting of a girl interrupted at her music, turned momentarily to look at you. The word "Vienna" was hastily penciled across the back of it.

I held the package reverently, as if its contents had assumed some sacramental value. I stood on the gravel path and watched her rise out of the tall slender chimney while the man from the crematorium gently spoke to me of elemental things, fire and ashes. With extended hand he indicated the Garden of Remembrance. He talked of urns and boxes, the aesthetics of death. People with bewildered looks mumbled condolences, took my hand. Kate had died instantly. I felt a perverse compulsion to picture the scene, to force myself to confront this horrible reality. It was what being a writer meant. You conjured up ghosts, you coined phrases, honed images, provided a story where none seemed to be. I imagined her sprawled on the tracks, I thought of the dust and oil on her cheek and shut my eyes against it. I wanted somehow to cup my hands around the body of my wife, to gather her to me, pull her away from this sordid world beneath the surface of the city. How fragile Kate was, how prone she was to colds and aches, how she shrank away from me at times, and when I thought of her being crushed by the wheels of a train I winced and cringed, as if I had sliced my tongue with a knife.

How long would it go on?

I dreaded staying on in the house, moving back into my routine: the morning drive along the twisting country roads; the hours at my desk putting words on a page. I feared the sense of incompleteness, as if a limb had been amputated. I thought of her things, her books, her photographs, now forever altered, their significance skewed. I considered the silence of the three rooms, the darkness and quiet broken only by the ringing of the telephone, the distant thunder.

There seemed to remain something of Kate woven into the texture of my life, slowly uncoiling and dispersing like smoke from a cigarette. I sensed it whenever I came in from outside, from the damp of autumn, and taking the first step inside the house I would pause and listen as if there were the slightest chance that in the cracks between the periods of silence I might hear some small distant voice caught forever in the floorboards, in the seams of the wallpaper. The density of the air seemed to change, the way sounds decayed, and more than once I heard myself whispering her name.

Day succeeded day, the curve of my life flattening out like the moment of expiration displayed on a hospital monitor. The complexities in which I had spent so much of my time enmeshed, the questions and suppositions, fell away from me, while things beyond me, apart from me, even once-familiar things like clouds and the rustle of leaves, seemed charged with symbol and mystery. It was as though I had absented myself from life. I was losing touch, fading into a neutral background.

People who had grown close to me, stood with me at the funeral, friends and relatives, invited me to stay with them for a week or two afterwards. I knew exactly what this meant: the arched eyebrows and muted tones of other people's pity. I tried to make out the expression of her sister, her face veiled in grief. I pressed her hand, listened to her weep. I felt as if the power of words had suddenly and irredeemably left me.

I thought of traveling great distances, of losing myself in some other country, another language. For those left behind the vivid memory of a man mourning his wife would soon become nothing more than a vague recollection of a face, a name that seemed to ring a bell. "Reid . . . Reid," they would say, tapping their chins impatiently. I thought of deserts, islands, great cities, ancient cities. The names Alexandria and Bombay came to mind, the crowds, the unceasing noise, the urgent hum and rumbling that rose from the ground at night, the peppery smell of an eastern sky. You could lose yourself there, in the labyrinths, the back streets.

Later her sister told me that during her stay Kate had said little. She had seemed distant; there, but not quite there; oddly absent. She said: "I didn't know Kate all that well. We were never close. I don't even know why she came to see me. I mean she never did, not without you anyway. She was so different. It was always like that. We never really got on. I don't know why she came to stay with Julian and me. Would you please say something?"

Josie worked at the British Tourist Authority on Fifty-seventh Street; her husband was with Shell Oil. They had been living in New York a year when Kate left England with me. People who had attended the funeral drifted in and out of the living room, picking at the platters of sliced meat. The coffee had run out, and no one troubled to refill the urn.

Later it would come to me: three or four times before this Kate had told me she had flown to New York to see her sister.

She got us each a drink. Julian and their son Andrew sat in the corner intent on a football game on the television. This was the first extended conversation I had ever had with my sister-in-law; undoubtedly the last. Josie sipped her drink; she said, "I could see she was upset about something. She didn't make much sense. She said something about feeling trapped." She looked at me and then turned away, towards the window. Central Park lay in shadow.

"Go on," I said.

"She was enjoying her work, she said, she liked translating whatever it was she was supposed to be doing. She was working hard, but then of course she always worked hard. She," and Josie looked at me.

I said: "Yes, go on."

"Perhaps she was seeing someone else."

"Someone else."

"Another man. She wasn't very specific about anything. There was something on her mind, though. I got the sense that she was seeing someone. You knew this, then? Or that you were seeing someone and she'd found out. Maybe that was it. Were you seeing anyone else?"

"Just keep talking."

"Are you seeing someone?"

"I said go on."

"She said she felt the need to do something. Anything. So she came to stay with us."

"And did what?"

There was a pause. "The usual sorts of things, I suppose. Went for walks, went to museums, shopped."

"And then she left."

"For Boston, I should think," Josie said.

"You should think? Why should you think, why shouldn't you know, what did she say?"

"I just assumed it was where she was going."

"You didn't offer to drive her to the airport?"

"She told me not to bother. She insisted on going alone."

"So she was coming back to me. She was coming home."

"She didn't exactly say that. She said she'd thought things over and was going back."

"To me."

"She didn't say."

"Just going back."

"That's it."

A STRAND
OF PEARLS

Of course Kate never went with me to Paris, had never intended
to. Our conversation at the restaurant was nothing more than a
kind of game, a mild flirtation, wholly artificial. Yet behind the
social camouflage, amidst the thicket of conversation, something
more interesting was going on.

In fact she turned me down flat. Wishful thinking is just another
genre of fiction.

Later she told me that other authors she had edited, and not
just the American ones, had been far more imaginative in their
propositions.

And had she ever once succumbed?

I watched the light in her eyes change.

I said to her: "Seriously, I'd like to see you again."

"I don't think so."

"Busy?"

"Oh yes."

"Do you eat dinner?"

"Every evening," she said.

"I'm only asking you to have a meal with me."

"I know."

"It won't be so bad."

"But."

"I can go on like this for hours," I warned her.

We did meet a second time, a few days after that first lunch near the museum: because I didn't know where to go, Kate chose a little bistro in Covent Garden Market. Again we met at her office. By then I had completed my interviews.

She said, "When are you leaving?"

I looked at her.

"For Paris."

Ah.

"I told you, I won't go unless you'll join me."

"No."

"Is that your final word?"

She smiled.

She was in perfect possession of herself: as we made our way through the lunchtime crowd on Long Acre she walked with confidence, she looked me in the eye when we talked, she smiled as if she meant it. I was caught by her, by the way she simultaneously intimidated and beguiled me, as one becomes hopelessly addicted at the first rush of a powerful narcotic.

"I think there's a problem here," I said as we waited to cross the street. "I think you're failing to take me seriously," and she burst forth with a lovely rich laugh and touched my arm.

She struck me at once with the complexity of her personality. She was like a coin, suddenly and unexpectedly revealing another side to herself.

She spoke of her translating and her growing distaste for her present work. "For a while I had my heart set on being an artist, a painter like my mother, but," and she let it drop. "Then I

thought about becoming a writer." She shrugged. "I suppose ed-
iting authors is a way for me to do it vicariously. But I've tried it
and I can't write, I can't even get close to it, not even past the
first sentence." She smiled and lit a cigarette and tossed her head
back, clearing her face of her thick blond hair. "I thought your
opening sentence was splendid," she said. "I always know if I'm
going to like a book by its opening."

"I don't believe you."

She laughed, she said, "No, really."

"It's not a particularly good first sentence. It's not what you
might call spectacular."

"That's why it's so good. It's so matter-of-fact in what it says.
But I like the tone of it, I like your confidence in understating
things. I like the danger of it, the way you leave things up to your
readers." She shrugged. "It can all go one way or another. I love
that ambiguity." She fell suddenly silent and then looked up at
me. "I do, you know."

It was late afternoon. We sat on the terrace outside the restaurant, under a large blue umbrella bearing the name Campari.
In mild bewilderment tourists milled about the marketplace with
its shops and street theatricals, jugglers and magicians and mimes,
so desperately colorful in this sinking city of grey. A man tossed
plastic Indian clubs in the air, one two three four, and I watched
his eyes as they followed the trajectories, the toss and tumble, I
watched his feet as they kept him steady, shifting suddenly this
way and that. Farther down a young man performed magic tricks
with hoops and wands and colored silk handkerchiefs. A large
audience began to gather. He'd found a girl he fancied and directed
his patter her way. His jokes were crude, the tricks obvious. He
asked the girl to step forward and fix handcuffs to his wrists. Now
things were beginning to get interesting.

Now the juggler had five clubs moving through the air. Kate
and I said nothing. An elderly woman standing near us said, "I

never saw such a thing in all me life." And then suddenly he stood stock-still, his hands by his sides, and let the clubs fall, five four three two, and I turned to look at her as she sat back in her chair, holding her wine glass, smiling to herself: utterly composed in her pleasure as she waited for the last club to drop.

‡   ‡   ‡

We saw each other again the next evening. And every succeeding evening. She said: "I must tell you that I don't want to get involved. You'll be returning to the States and there's just."

Yes?

"There's no future in it."

When I left the hotel a week later she asked me to move in with her, "just for a week or two," she said. "Just to see how things work out."

She was due some time off from the office and wanted to show me around London. We could take the train up to Cambridge. I thought of renting a car. But Paris was out. "Not now. Not this time," she said.

She lived in a flat just south of Belsize Park, within walking distance of Hampstead. What had once been someone's house had been converted into a number of apartments. A single staircase wound its way to the top floors. The walls were so thick you could hear nothing of your neighbors. Now it was about to be modernized and the apartments sold off. Kate had to vacate by the end of August.

She stood and watched as I looked around the living room. There was a table with a vase of flowers on it, a bowl of fruit. A small sofa. A television on a metal cart. On the floor was a faded Oriental rug that had belonged to her parents. On the wall a print of a woman holding a balance between the thumb and forefinger of her right hand. Propped on the mantel were invitations, postcards from museums. I lifted the lid of her turntable and read the label of the record. When I reached the window I turned to look at her.

Her rooms overlooked the back garden, a weedy jungle that over years of neglect had strangled within its growth an old wicker chair. Bees hovered about the heads of wildflowers, moved off to others. You could hear the birds in the trees. There was a stillness in the air. It seemed impossible that a city lay at her door.

"Of course there isn't much of a kitchen." She opened the fridge. "There isn't much food, either. We'll go out to the market later."

I stood in the doorway of the bedroom, I said, "It's like your living room. Neat. Tidy." I looked at her. "Spartan."

"I don't like clutter," she said, brushing past me to make the bed.

Beyond the window the sky was growing cloudy and leaves began to rustle in the wind. Next to the desk a narrow set of bookshelves held an assortment of paperbacks, novels and poetry in French, dictionaries. A photograph of her and her parents taken on her sixth birthday stood on top of it.

Over her bed was another Vermeer, a woman standing at a table, looking at her reflection in the mirror by the window, tying a strand of pearls around her neck, her lips slightly parted, her eyebrows raised: a moment of such privacy that it forbade interpretation. I looked at Kate and smiled and then she came to me and held me against her, as though she had suddenly been overcome with a terrible loneliness. We hadn't yet slept together. Yet she demanded the physical intimacy of held hands, embraces. We stood very still by the side of her bed, the smoky haze of afternoon filling the window. Quietly she said: "I never take risks, you know."

"Neither do I," I said, and she pulled away and stared at me as though I had betrayed her. Of course I took risks, all the time, but only when I was writing; I could be courageous only on the

page. Though I had never lifted a hand in anger, rarely shouted a
threat or plotted revenge, in my books people played out their
obsessions in black rain-wet alleys, in seedy basement nightclubs
where strangers turned to look at them. They held guns to their
heads, surrendered to their darker impulses. Anonymous people
telephoned and gave warning; the same car appeared and reappeared, trailing the protagonist, mapping out the direction of his
life.

That afternoon we made love. Her hair hung loose as she rose
and fell above me, her eyes shutting as she lifted her face.

Kate said that it had been a year since she'd last been to bed
with a man, a writer she'd been working with. They had been
talking of marriage, and then she found out he was already married,
with a wife and daughter not half a mile away. Since then she'd
been reluctant to get involved. "But I don't want to grow cold,"
she said. "I just don't want to," and she left her sentence unfinished.

I watched her as she dressed, as she sat on the edge of the bed
and brushed her hair in the diffuse light of dusk and then stopped
brushing and turned to me, her eyes wide, a different person.

A woman weighs gold and pearls.

A woman puts on a necklace, looks into a mirror.

These were the hieroglyphs of our life.

A PUZZLE

I took a semester-long leave of absence from the college where I taught and went away for a few weeks, first stopping to see my mother in Hartford. I hadn't been there in over a year. She only knew of Kate's death because I called her doctor at the nursing home and he had taken it upon himself to tell her a few days before I arrived, calmly and simply, as if describing something complex to a small child. I imagined Kate becoming a hastily drawn stick figure, descending to the subway in the flat, monochromatic world of a cartoon panel.

The noise of the traffic drove me insane. The people seemed ugly, hostile, the buildings anonymous, reflecting back my own face in polished steel, endless windows. At first my mother failed to recognize me. She ate her meals in silence, sitting with her knees apart, enraptured by her television, her soap operas, the endless bizarre parade of talk shows; dozing with her hands in her lap; waking with a start whenever I tried to switch off the set. This was not the woman who played Twenty Questions with me when I was seven years old and bored, who would tell me stories of her youth as a chorus girl on Broadway who frequented speak-easies and had once met Legs Diamond. Something had diminished her, reduced her to becoming just another stranger. Old men and women with jittery fingers roamed the corridors, babbling to them-selves, crying out names, summoning up the dead.

In the grey of afternoon my mother became lucid and wondered aloud whether I would ever remarry.

I said, "It's a little soon for that, don't you think?" and my mother told me it was never too soon, I wasn't getting any younger, the world wasn't going to stop revolving for me. I had turned thirty-five a week before Kate had left me and I could no longer bear the weight of proverbs.

She treated me as if I were diseased, struck with something fatal; as if for her to acknowledge my wife's death would open a wound, create contagion. She never mentioned her name, reducing Kate to the condition of pronoun.

We watched the news together on her television. An elderly landlady had been found robbed and brutally murdered in a board-inghouse on the north side, her skull crushed by a heavy object, possibly the blunt end of a small axe or hatchet. A man of no fixed address had been arrested, having been discovered wandering about a house just outside New Britain. When questioned by police he claimed to be a land surveyor the owners had hired the day before. The body that had been taken out of the river on Tuesday had been identified as, and then I noticed my mother had fallen asleep. Two days later I packed my bag and left the hotel in the city center. At the airport bar I sipped beer and watched the screen as arrivals and departures were announced. I thought of going to London. I liked London, Kate and I both had friends there, it was where we had met, where we had lived together for a summer. I thought of returning to the house, looking up at our window as one views again a favorite film just to recapture particular scenes.

There was San Francisco with its evening mists. Montreal. I had been to Prague, Jerusalem, Amsterdam. Then there was Paris . . . But I couldn't go to Paris, not now, perhaps not ever. Not without Kate. I watched the cities appear on the screen, L.A. Mexico City. Rio. Berlin. Sometimes I could not seem to sit still, remain in one place very long.

Kate was just the opposite. For most of her life she had stayed close to home. At Cambridge she attended Girton College and during vacations slept in the same bedroom at her aunt's house where she had passed much of her childhood, where she had cultivated her imagination. She took me to see her old college. We walked through the apple orchard that was part of the campus, moving along the straight rows of new-mown grass. She knelt down by a tree and looked at me as she had that first time in the restaurant, as if I were a stranger, someone with whom she was conducting business. "That's where I would sit on warm days, reading," and she grasped a branch of the tree, an intimate, exquisitely private part of her life.

That was what had drawn me to her: the sheer fresh oppositeness of her. I was all words; she aspired to silence and stillness. And unexpectedly I smiled as I thought of it.

Perhaps she was seeing someone else, Josie had said.

‡   ‡   ‡

I stood in the lobby of the deserted hotel and signed my name on the little yellow card. We had first gone to Italy just before we returned to the States. Jokingly we called it a honeymoon. We rented a Fiat in Milan and drove from one town to the next, eventually reaching the nightmare that is Venice in August. We had been married a week earlier at the Kensington Registry Office during Kate's lunch hour. It was the sort of thing you read about in a Graham Greene novel: our witness was the man who had come to repair the wiring.

Memory collided with memory, the distant past with the recent.

Now, less than two weeks after Kate's death, I was staying in the same small hotel in a village near Parma, my window overlooking the town square, a fountain. Occasionally a crippled dog or an elderly man would hobble into view. The young dark-haired chambermaid flirted with me, giving me sly looks as she passed by in the empty corridors, brushing against me. Perhaps the recollection of that earlier time, when Kate and I seemed so suited to each other, like two halves of a puzzle, helped me regain my balance. I took long walks in the countryside. For the first time since Kate's death I thought of writing, wondering how I could return to it, what words would draw me into a story; what story I could possibly tell. Friends and professional contacts urged me to go back to work, immerse myself in a novel. But I could only get as far as the opening sentence.

I remembered the night she left me.

I wondered how Kate would have aged. I thought of her as I knew her, as I would always think of her: slim, blond, lean. Her beauty was not the simple flashiness of an adolescent or a Hollywood starlet, but rather the complexity that comes with maturity and intelligence, impossible to characterize.

Once a month she would drive into Boston and have her hair neatly cut an inch above the shoulders at a hairdresser's on Newbury Street. I imagined her sitting in the chair, watching the transformation in the mirrored wall, pleased with what she had been, with what she was becoming. She would spend the day in town, have lunch, do some shopping, go to a museum. She would come home with clothes and books and records and interesting new foods, and then she would try on her things, skirts, trousers, blouses. And I would sit and nod and smile, because she had superb taste in everything. I thought of her as cool and angular.

I closed my eyes as I thought of her in my room overlooking the fountain. Now she was frozen in my imagination, ageless, and this agelessness seemed a kind of purity to me. It was Kate become idea, no longer a person; conceivable only in the abstract. Her death had released her from the passage of time, plucked her from the narrative of her life. I looked at the postcard I'd found in her coat pocket. Without seeing me the woman who had turned from her music stared into my eyes.

The distance between us was becoming terrifying.

I kept my eyes shut and tried to reconstruct my wife. I thought of her hands, graceful and slim. I loved sitting at the table, watching her maneuver her knife and fork, her fingers lifting a glass, sketching a rare unexpected gesture; feeling them at rest against my face, cool and certain in their touch.

Her neck, long and smooth and pale in the moonlight.

A voice like warm milk.

Keep going.

The shape of her chin, the certainty of it, the definition.

I thought of the delicate folds of flesh at the groin, the little curves that framed her smile, a freckle on her throat. I would watch her wash, dress, brush her hair, naked before the mirror, tilting her head to the side. The way she said my name: *David.* She gently tossed her head, like so, setting her hair in motion, looking at me as if seeking her reflection in my face, demanding it to be there. I forced myself to see her this way, pink and alive and warm.

Details kept returning to me: never the woman herself, never Kate in all her totality. Death was a cubist, breaking the deceased into separate planes, shattering her in my memory into light and shadow.

"How calm you are," she would say to me, touching my arm, not quite certain I was there. "How calm, how steady."

Cool and angular.

"Say something."

My eyes remained on her.

Go on.

"Say something."

I opened my eyes and she disappeared.

I shut off the light and went to bed. I woke at three and drank some mineral water. Though I had been there only four days, I had spent enough time away. I knew I had to go home, get it over with, as if I were on that same train which had run Kate down, as if I needed to move headlong into a time when grief was behind me, when I had come to terms with my loss. I felt as if I were suffocating, as though a great weight were pressing upon my lungs, impeding breath. It seemed pointless not to come home. No matter how painful it would be I could not avoid returning to the routine of my life.

I would not lack for companions. After the funeral neighbors and friends and colleagues at the college had offered me company, help, meals. They looked at me as though I had been on a long journey to an unexplored region, some distant planet. I heard from support groups based in three different towns. Somehow they had got my name, undoubtedly they had read the obituary in the local paper. They told me there were other widowers in the area, men who were begging to be heard, who needed to listen to the grief and troubles of others. We would sit in a circle and reach out to each other. There would be coffee to drink and doughnuts to eat and bonds to be formed. Reading lists would be distributed. In time we would grow articulate. A young woman from a church group called and asked me if Jesus was in my heart, she demanded that I join her in prayer, she spoke of salvation and damnation, of the pain and smoke of hell; but there was nothing in my heart, it was a hollow, a place of echoes. I was contacted by dating services. One woman rang and said: "I understand you are now no longer married, Mr. Reid. There are many women in the greater Boston area who are dying to meet a man in your position."

The Authors Guild wrote asking for my annual dues.

I opened the window overlooking the little square and felt the air on my face. It was like this every night. Always at three: my mind turning to Kate.

She used to wake also, lift a hand, touch my shoulder. When she turned in bed, I turned as well, curved an arm around her, cupped her bare breast.

Two halves of a puzzle.

MOONLIGHT

She appears again, the woman who weighs pearls and gold in the afternoon, in other works by the artist, scenes of quiet drama, interrupted moments. Women look up from their work or recreation, disturbed by your prying eyes; servants deliver letters: in a civilization that finds its watersheds in the great upheavals of history, revolutions and wars and ideological shifts, these are only insignificant events, seeds of consequence that yet linger enigmatically for years, centuries, forever.

A woman stands by a window reading a letter. Another is absorbed in the making of lace. Still another looks at you accusingly as you distract her from her music lesson. A woman is putting on her pearl necklace: caught but evasive, *You will never know me,* she says, slipping away from comprehension.

Of course there's always a trade-off, an infernal covenant demanding your signature: for the permanence of art, the loss of soul. The women in the paintings possess no life beyond the four walls of their frames. Each canvas is a window, each scene frozen, like a distant memory held fast in an old man's brain.

But it's not a window.

A woman sits at a table covered with a rug, or cloth of rich brocade. Three men, all in an apparent state of intoxication, hover expectantly nearby. We are in the midst of a potentially lurid tale. Lewd, lascivious, lecherous and libidinous, the adjectives tumble onto the page.

The woman seems more substantial, ruddier and sturdier; yet it's obvious she's the same woman who weighs pearls and gold in the dwindling hours of a Dutch afternoon. Now it's nighttime and she's playing the procuress. The light is poor, the thick fabrics and dark walls forbid illumination. This is a world of whispers and forthright looks, of groping hands and furtive embraces, of flesh and damp hollows, a place where senses are acute and things happen behind shut doors. But she can look after herself, the procuress, she can hold her drink, she's accustomed to hearing the raw words of men on the make. In her left hand is a half-empty glass of wine. It's the way she grips it that catches the attention. As if she were holding something thick and stiff and alive, and our eyes are drawn to it as readily as they are to a flash of nudity in an uncurtained window.

What is happening here? Can this be the same woman who, pregnant and demure, weighs gold and pearls on a late autumn afternoon? Does the woman who holds the balance have a second career, are we being exposed to another, wholly unexpected, side to her character? Does she come home, change her clothes, light the lamps and admit strange men into her parlor?

In a word: is she moonlighting?

Her right hand no longer weighs coins, but rests open against the table, waiting for the man to pay for his pleasure: the rake whose hand blithely encompasses her left breast as he stands close behind her, transforming a simple transaction into a moment of wanton intimacy. He's a ladies' man, no doubt, dressed to the nines for his night out with the boys. He's also the best-looking of the trio, and he knows it. He wears his hat at a jaunty angle, low over his brow. His jacket is deep red; it stands out in a crowd, it reflects handsomely in the shimmer of a canal. Certainly he has lovers, other men's wives. You can imagine him on a sultry August afternoon while someone's husband is away on business. You can see him in the bedroom, in a mood of calm detachment, gazing down at her exposed breasts. A shaft of sunlight strikes the floor near the chair. A broom leans against the corner. Through the open doorway we can see the kitchen: a table, a chair. The woman gasps and, clenching her jaw, presses herself to him. Now it's time to go. He dresses, adjusts his hat, touches her cheek, bids farewell.

This is not a man of art: we read him all too easily, his life is only as deep as his smile, the way he grasps the woman's breast. At heart he is unscrupulous and weak, he knows nothing of love, life holds no mysteries for him.

Now it's evening and a sliver of gold shines from between the thumb and forefinger of his right hand. It's almost as if he's weighing the two: a guilder, a breast.

The woman's composure as she conducts the business of the night: our attention is caught by the serenity of her expression. She sits at the center of the universe, she dwarfs the men seeking quick anonymous moments of joy.

It was a fairly common theme in art back then, a visit to the brothel. Vermeer even owned a painting called *The Procuress*, by another artist, one Dirck van Baburen. Other painters had tackled the subject. One might even say that the world of art was one vast whorehouse. But there's something different about this one: the artist himself has come to the bordello, and so have we, because he sees us, the smiling man seated at the left, he stares us straight in the eye, immersed in deep shadow, somehow outside the scene, as if he were a minor character in someone else's drama. Grinning uncertainly as if he has just missed the point of a salacious joke. He's barely touched his wine. Now he is about to have a drink.

He holds his glass up to us: *skaal!*

But things are not as simple as all that. He knows he is looking out at us, he hoped he would be when he painted himself in 1656, for although it is the woman who catches our eye with her glowing self-confidence and reassuring smile, though we know she would be safe and strong even among rogues and murderers, this painting is the equivalent of a first-person narrative, and the artist is saying, *I may paint the pictures, but their meaning is beyond me.*

The point is that he *has* missed the point.

Then there's the woman: we've seen her many times before and we'll see her again and again in other situations. Perhaps he's missed other things as well: one senses a betrayal in his life, something going on right under his nose.

August. A warm afternoon. He's gone off to buy paints.

Consider it.

It's not a window. It's a mirror.

Only one person is aware of us, the artist himself, smiling with alarming merriment at our sudden discomfort. He can almost read our minds: are we looking through a window, are we meant to be in the room . . . ?

If the man holding the drink, sitting in the shadows, is a self-portrait, then Vermeer probably was looking into a mirror set up alongside his canvas, shifting his eyes from one to the other, adding details, painting that strange silly face that grins out at us with sinister vividness from three centuries earlier.

So we're a mirror, a simple piece of furniture in the household inventory of the procuress. Of course she needs one there: her girls must check their coiffures from time to time, their pouts. Her customers need to adjust their hats, arrange those curls that fall so elegantly to their shoulders.

And we're nothing but reflection. His bafflement is our confusion.

What happens afterwards? Undoubtedly two or three young
women in a state of deshabille are summoned. Undoubtedly the
coxcomb in red predictably thinks aloud, *I like the one with the big
arse; I bet she's got a tight one.* And of course he pinches their thighs,
hefts their breasts. His friend gets second choice; the artist, of
course, by nature a voyeur, isn't even there.

Or else nothing happens. The man still waits; his friend exists
in a condition of perpetual inebriation. The artist holds his glass
aloft, looking out at us as though from another world, some
intermediate state between life and art. The woman's palm remains
open, waiting for the coin to fall. Everything has been reduced to
a state of expectancy, all pleasure deferred. There will be no
betrayal. There is no afterwards. Chaos will not ensue. It is an
endless condition of To Be Continued.

6

L A C E

Sometimes I wondered if life was a weave of echo and reflection: words and images forming patterns across the years, creating the texture of memory; hinting at some greater matrix.

A weave, a vast web built high in the corner of a room reeking of dust and old wood, the antique odor of solitude, of emptiness.

A web, an intricate fragile palace of tidy little connections, causes and effects, hidden stairways and dark alcoves, rooms that lead to rooms that lead to rooms. Silent rooms without views, locked rooms. Eventually you returned to the beginning; eventually you ran out of doors and steps and hallways.

A web: the way thoughts moved nimbly about the brain, setting off sparks in the imagination. Thoughts, images, memories, all linked together. Like a globe: the image came to me: like a detailed globe, each longitude and latitude carefully drawn, thin lines of ink joining hemispheres: the world in a net, a captive fish. A net, a globe, a web.

A fly on a summer afternoon, suddenly caught, each struggling movement trapping it further.

Bzz.

I saw Kate again about eight weeks after she died: as though she had never left me. Not quite: as though she had left me and not died; and I wondered which was the more painful, the eternal irreversible loss of her or the ache of knowing she was with someone else.

A woman stands by a window, reading a letter, and I can't make out a word of it.

A man goes into a hotel, sees things.

Things began to grow complicated.

Let me go back to the beginning.

The evening I returned from Italy the phone was ringing as I turned the key in the lock. I stood in the darkness and held the receiver to my ear and listened to silence.

Not the absolute silence of a dead line, but the layered stillness of someone's mute presence. I could detect a shallow breathing, as if whoever was there were listening intently to me, awaiting a word that might break the tension, liberate him. The two of us breathed in unison and waited.

It was odd being alone. Things usually unnoticed, overheard conversations, the lingering stares of strangers, dead telephone calls, even the sudden thick quiet of the house: all seemed to take on an obscure importance, as if they were signs requiring interpretation. And so I was not alone, because these things were with me always.

A spider in the bath; a red stain on the rug.

Someone in a passing car laughed, and my memory turned to ice.

I hung up the phone and began switching on the lights in all the rooms. Even before unpacking I had a drink and listened to Bach and shut my eyes and gave myself up to the cool mathematical structures, lines of melody and countermelody that seemed to form themselves into knots before unraveling. Perhaps this was the essence of art, I sometimes thought, this tension between entanglement and release; and yet when I listened to music and when I leafed through the album of Vermeer's paintings Kate had given me a month before she died and often when I wrote I would feel myself pressing up against a wall or membrane whose dimensions and density were unknown to me, a web of speculation: as if, being hunted, I were seeking an open window, a door that might open, a gap.

I stood in the doorway and thought of how much she had loved it here, how we used to cross the road and walk together down to the lake, the dead leaves crackling beneath our feet. The quiet when we got there, the still surface of water. Now it was autumn again, most of the leaves had turned shades of red and yellow, the air was thick with the odors of moist earth and decomposition, and the lake rippled in the wind.

When I met her I had been living here about six months. I had been offered a job teaching required English courses to students at a nearby art college. I enjoyed going there three times a week, I savored the smells of acrylics and oils, plasticene, turpentine. The air was filled with cigarette smoke and the girls were pretty as they walked barefoot down the corridors, their long hair swinging behind them.

I was expendable, I knew nothing of drawing or painting or the baroque politics of the art world. I would sometimes watch my colleagues at their easels, working the paint into the canvas with their palette knives, swearing in whispers, struggling to defeat this whiteness. They walked about in stained blue jeans and chambray shirts, their fingers covered with smears of dried paint, and they tolerated me whose hands were always clean.

The house was set off the road on an acre of land, much of it densely wooded, at the edge of the wetlands. I rented it from a couple who owned an adjoining horse farm. Just off a large kitchen was a small living room and our bedroom, where Kate worked. My desk was in the living room.

We had always dreamed of buying a larger place, something more elaborate, near the coast perhaps, with a columned portico and circular drive and a swimming pool. Sometimes she imagined the two of us achieving a certain eminence in our professions, growing old, greeting the children when they came in for Christmas or a week in summer.

Possibly because her death was so sudden I found it difficult to remember Kate as part of a narrative, as someone who moved fluidly through time and space. I saw her rather in a series of tableaux, in still pictures, as if my memory were an album I could leaf through whenever I wished, as though to remember my wife I were forced to move from one photograph to another, fixing her in her various moods and aspects of her personality; unable to fit them together.

Until the night I returned I had tried to avoid Kate's desk, untouched since the day she had left me: her appointment diary and address book, some pens, books, letters to be answered; the few pieces of mail she had received after her death, still unopened, letters from publishers and journals which continued to arrive as though nothing had happened.

Before her death I had always respected her privacy; since her funeral I had simply avoided her things, ignoring them as though they were no longer there. When I needed something from the closet I would push her clothes off to the side, holding my breath against her scent, terrified of memory. Yet I could throw away nothing that had belonged to her, not her clothes, not the half-empty bottles that stood on a shelf in the bathroom, the facial cleansers, the moisturizers. Even their names had assumed some obscure power over me: Lancôme, Clarins, Laszlo.

The irrational thought came to me that perhaps something of

the soul survives in the material belongings of a person. A dress, a book, a wallet, a shoe, a torn photograph, things, rubbish, gold. It exerts its influence on us, warns us away, surrounds something as simple as a bar of chocolate or a magazine with a kind of protective spell.

As if I expected her to walk in at any moment, reclaim her possessions, slip back into life.

I looked at her desk that night I returned from Italy. Everything was as it had been that evening she left me. *I just need to get away for a while,* she had said. I could leave everything the way it was and live with the unseen presence of Kate, not as if she were somehow there, lingering ghostlike in a dark corner or passing through the rooms like an icy breeze, but more as a pressure I could feel on my brain, the heat of fever, the sense of a tumor. Or I could bring this to an end, this anguish, the endless speculation that filled my mind.

I leaned back in her chair and looked at the little brass clock Kate kept at the corner of her desk. It had run down and I hadn't bothered to wind it, and so it remained forever four twenty-five. She loved objects: metal boxes with hinged lids, things made of papier-mâché, inkwells and paperweights. Each was placed just so, alone on a table or grouped with others, the significance of it known only to her.

I began by setting aside all the papers connected to her work: correspondence from publishers, journals. I was astonished to see how disorganized she was. Two of her desk drawers were nearly impossible to open for all the papers that had been jammed into them. Most of these were old and useless, they quickly filled the wastebasket. The drawer just beneath the desktop was strewn with paperclips and rubber bands and old, useless pens, more letters. It seemed so unlike Kate: tidy Kate with never a hair out of place. I gathered all the bits and pieces together, the clips and erasers and pencils, and transferred them to my own desk. I began to sift through the letters: she still kept up with friends from her school and university days.

A pale blue envelope lay at the bottom of one of the drawers. It was addressed by hand to her. It had been posted in New York three days before she left me. It had been torn open.

There was no letter.

I reached forward and switched on her computer. I looked at the screen and began reading through the translation she'd been working on when she died, a novel by the French writer Marc Rougemont. I read listlessly, as if a great fatigue had suddenly overcome me.

> *A man walked into a hotel. The city was in the grip of a heatwave.*
>
> > *Night fell. Midnight arrived.*
> > *Time passed.*
> > *He stood in his room and poured himself another drink. It was a warm evening and he unbuttoned his shirt. He put down his glass and switched off the lamp and parted the curtains. A man and a woman entered a room in the building across the road.*

In reading the words Kate had chosen I felt both guilty and aroused, as if in the nighttime I had spied a woman undressing in a window: as if I had caught Kate suddenly off guard.

I looked at the envelope, I thought of the postcard she had left in her coat pocket; *Vienna.* I felt as if I were becoming enmeshed in some plot of my own design, further trapping myself the more I thought of Kate, the more I mourned her.

The man watching them picked up the phone.

I turned off the machine and walked to the closet and took down her clothes, armfuls of them, and laid them on the bed. I pulled the drawers from her bureau and emptied out sweaters and stockings and lacy underwear. Two hours earlier my plane was descending into Boston, defining circles over the city and the bay, and I sat there exhausted with the other tourists, dying for a good night's sleep. Now I felt awake, alert, gripped by necessity. I began to fill large plastic rubbish bags with her dresses and underwear and cosmetics and then I loaded up the Saab with them and drove out into the rain.

I couldn't seem to place precisely when it first appeared. It was impossible to see the driver's face in the darkness. He must have picked me up somewhere near the house. I regretted having gone this way. The narrow road twisted and curved as it followed the contour of the lake. He was close enough to me so that his headlights reflected back on his blue Mercedes, and he remained behind me, though there were any number of turns he could have taken.

Being followed.

I smiled to myself because it seemed so preposterous, so alien to my world. Not to my fiction, where everyone at one time or another was followed, but to the insular quiet world I inhabited. *Absurd:* my lips formed the word itself.

I tapped the brake pedal, slowed down. Being followed: it was like something out of a novel or a film, and I actually laughed aloud in the way I sometimes did when ill at ease. We must have traveled this way for nearly four miles, past darkened gas stations and fried-fish stands and ice cream parlors, through one town and then another, linked by his obsession. I got onto the interstate and headed north. I thought of Kate's things in the trunk and for a moment felt as if I were transporting a corpse in some elaborate denouement to a crime. Was the person in the Mercedes to become my accomplice? Or a silent witness who would dog my steps until I broke down, surrendered to his demands? This is how my mind works. Wheels within wheels.

The highway was oddly deserted. For a mile or so the Mercedes kept its distance, so that it was only two small headlights behind me, and then it came closer, so close that I was forced to change lanes, and even then it stayed behind me. It played with me, moving just ahead and then falling behind; withdrawing and approaching. There was nowhere I could go, the four wide lanes seeming to narrow as the exits grew farther apart. During the day you couldn't drive without seeing the police: hidden beyond a turn, emanating radar beams; flying low in a helicopter, watching, waiting, linked by radio to headquarters; patrolling the passing lane, disguised as late-model Fords, sinister and impassive behind their Ray-Bans. *Bastards,* you'd say as they fingered you over. Now that I needed them there was nothing: no law, no one to help, no sanctuary on a wet autumn night.

I turned on my directionals, I switched lanes, and then suddenly the Mercedes sped up and began to pass me so closely that I had no choice but to veer off the road onto the breakdown lane. By the time I turned to look it was gone. It struck me: I could have been killed. I felt my heart racing, my scalp prickling, and in my mind I could almost hear the insane laughter as he clocked off the miles between us.

How calm you are, she had once said to me.

How calm, how steady.

I drove until I found a rest area near the New Hampshire border. I took the bags from the trunk and stuffed them into the rubbish barrels, among the discarded skin mags, the oozing condoms, the beer cans and uneaten remains of junk food. I could have neatly folded and stacked her clothes, given them to the Salvation Army, the people who lived in cardboard boxes. But this was no time for charity. Kate was dead.

BAD NEWS

Now she's standing by an open window, reading a letter. It's impossible to tell from her expression what the news is. Is someone coming to visit? Has her husband or lover been delayed in his travels?

Or has she just received a bit of bad news . . . ?

Her eyebrows are lifted, her lips barely parted: it's as if she's about to say something to herself, the merest whisper of a commentary. A gasp, a sigh, a sudden intake of breath? Possibly a word, a man's name. Too loud, and everyone in the street will hear.

Shh.

It's bad news. It must be. Her heart seems to have come to a stop. Her lover has just informed her that her husband is onto him. As he has gone about his business in Delft a man has been tailing him, from alley to shop to customhouse to lute maker's a man continually follows him. When he goes into a tavern for a drink, a figure stands at the window, watching. When he posts a letter, a man appears and then quickly hides behind a tree. At night, as he looks out his window one last time before retiring, someone steps from a darkened doorway and walks away.

This has become a motif in his life.

So now it's our turn to watch, yet we're not meant to be aware of the woman and her predicament: that's all beyond us. It's a classic arrangement: a woman in profile, standing, holding a page between her hands (her knuckles white, the tension all too evident). On the table in the foreground a bowl of fruit lying on a now-familiar rug. But what Vermeer wants us to stand back and admire is the way he has captured a reflection of the woman's face in the leaded panes of glass. See, he has even broken up the image, faithful to the realism of four separate pieces of glass, unevenly set in their panes.

Step closer, look for yourself.

The woman has a ghost. She is young and has her strength and yet already she possesses a phantom, a double, a fractured insubstantial image of herself reading the news in a letter. Is it an emblem of this separate life she has been leading? Or has she just lost something of herself? Perhaps we must rethink the contents of the letter. Clearly the news is worse than we'd expected, much worse. Possibly there has been a death in the family. Or else her lover has been found dead, stabbed behind some squalid public house, lying in a puddle with his only company the rats of Delft with their whiskers and tails and tiny excited voices.

Or it's something more complicated than that. Her lover must see her immediately. Woven into his phrases is a thread of violence, a sinister subtext that burdens her with guilt and the need for flight. Time is running out; desperation has gripped him: the drama of it is evident in his words, the way his phrases slither rapidly across the page, the splashes of ink here and there betraying his agitation. She must leave: her husband, her children. Now.

Maybe we're wrong. Perhaps the contents of the letter aren't our business. After all, we can't read the woman's mind. Reach out and touch her, go on; but you'll never get close to her. Never.

So whatever she's reading is up to us. Possibly it's good news. Her sister is going to have a baby after all. Wonderful! Or an old friend, a good friend, is coming up from Amsterdam to see the woman who stands by the window, reading a letter. It all depends on your state of mind. You see what you wish to see.

It's bad news, coming on a thundery summer afternoon.

I knew it.

The sickly yellowish light stinks of ozone, the low clouds churn and thicken over Delft. Fruit tumbles out of a platter on the table. It's a day when even the canals are unreflective, and the woman can think of only one thing: there is no way out. She has become trapped in a dilemma, between one person and another. The scales are no longer in balance: look how she holds the page, tightly between her hands. Her lips are open, she has grown pale, and when we stand back and look at her we see that in this room she is very small indeed. This isn't the woman holding the balance, or the procuress at her table: this woman is drowning amidst the walls and curtains and furniture, diminished by fear, bereft of possibility.

I had seen this before.

THREE SNAPSHOTS

1. She said it was her favorite photo. It's her sixth birthday. She's in the garden of her house in Cambridge, her hands behind her back, posing in her party dress, standing in a world of blacks and greys and a sooty white.

Catherine. Cathy.

Kate.

Her smile isn't that of a little girl; or rather, we can detect the adult beginning to form in her, the merest shadow of maturity, and it shows there, in her expression, the way she holds her mouth, the distance she keeps from her parents. Possibly it comes, as it so often does, from unhappiness.

They stand on either side of her and one step back: her father, a Cambridge don, a cigarette between his fingers, a look on his face that shows he isn't quite there: possibly he's mulling over some philosophical question, a problem in ethics or the existence of God. Her mother, a painter, stocky and cheerful and a little bohemian in a shapeless flowered dress, her open face and almost too-wide smile seeming to absorb much of the light. Perhaps it was she who had cut the bangs of my wife's hair at such an awkward slant, and I can see Kate sitting in a chair, squirming and whiny, saying, *Oh Mum, stop.*

Kate said: "Of course I don't remember my parents, not really. They're like blurs in a photograph, they passed through so quickly that I somehow missed them. Sometimes I look at it closely, I look at their expressions and think that in a funny way I can see it coming in their eyes."

"You mean——"

And she said: "Yes. That's what I mean."

Both of them were to die in a car accident six months later on their way back from London. Kate and her sister were at their Aunt Min's house in Linton, not far from Cambridge. They were waiting for Mum and Dad to pick them up; this was what bothered her most, she once told me: she could remember everything she did that day with Josie, every detail was set in her mind, the colors of things, the sounds, cloud formations, all fixed there retrospectively by the impending shock. They had been playing and then they had grown bored and they listened to a children's show on the radio and they had lunch and tea and by then they were orphans.

Such violence. Such art.

"It was an accident," she said. "My father lost control of the car and it swerved off the road."

We were in bed. We had just made love and then we began to talk. It was a late summer afternoon in London and we lay on our backs, sheetless, our hands barely touching. I watched her as she looked up at the ceiling, I ran my finger gently over the curve and rise of her dry lips.

She said: "I once heard a psychiatrist say there's no such thing as an accident." She propped herself on an elbow and looked beyond me.

"It's funny," she said. "I didn't know what had been going on, and then one day Josie said they'd been arguing a great deal lately, my parents. I must have somehow blanked it out. I used to think everything was bliss. But she was right, because my aunt eventually told me that my father had found out my mother was having an affair with a painter in London." Kate looked at me. "Apparently they used to have terrible rows. But I can't remember them."

"That's no reason to drive your car off the road."

And she looked at me.

Kate spoke of the photo only after I had been living with her for a month, only after she was certain of me. She said: "This photo is the dividing line of my life."

2. I'm a terrible photographer. I have no sense of composition. People appear too distant, dwarfed by the background, their expressions a remote mystery, a mess of smudges and shadows. Sometimes I capture only their extremities, an extended arm, a fragment of leg, half a head: the world as battlefield. Occasionally my finger appears: a dark, ominous thing disturbing the view. Only once did I have any success, and it was sheer chance, a simple accident, that the picture actually came out. It sits on my desk, in a silver frame. I took it the summer after we were married, when we were on vacation in Martha's Vineyard. We had ferried to Vineyard Haven and stayed a week at an inn in Chilmark. We rented bicycles and a sailboat and left our work behind us.

It was deep summer and, though there always seemed to be a stiff breeze, the air was unusually hot, almost tropical. We bought a kite, and after hurrying across the blue unbroken sky for the first time it fell into the sea, soundlessly crashing into the waves. Each afternoon Kate and I walked along the beach, sometimes stopping to sit in the sun.

I looked at her as she leaned back on her hands and watched

a group of children playing with a dog. We'd decided to put off having children until she had established herself as a translator: this was her condition, not mine. She sat at her desk often late into the night, working on Marc Rougemont's novel, worried she had lost her way in the thicket of words.

She said, "What beautiful children."

I wasn't sure we should have children, after all. I didn't feel I could be a competent parent. I had never been a particularly good son. Fatherhood struck me as a profound mystery. I worried the burden would be on Kate. I said, "Do you want to have some?"

She laughed and rested her hand on my knee. "Some? You mean more than one? Like a litter of kittens?"

I shrugged. "One, anyway."

"One is fine."

"All right."

"You mean you're ready to try?"

"If you are I am."

She smiled and looked out to sea, rocking her body forward as if a knot had come undone within her. And when she turned to look at me I pressed the shutter, capturing a brief glimpse of her last real happiness.

3. It was in the last days before she left me, and we were in the midst of a late heat wave. Because we were sheltered by the woods the breeze from the coast never reached us. The walls of our bedroom sweated, and odd stains, yellowish and elaborate, appeared on our ceilings, awaiting decipherment. At night, in the civilized stillness of the smaller hours, the reek of animal came through the windows, a ripe disturbing stink accompanied by the crazed whistling and screams of the beasts that roamed the area, raccoons and skunks coupling and warring in the darkness.

Sometimes helicopters passed low overhead, as if searching the

woods for renegades, or the decaying remains of people who had
fled or been taken or simply become lost. We lived close enough
to the lake so that when the trees were bare in the winter you
could see the sunlight shimmering on the water. We were near
enough the highway to be in Boston in half an hour. On some
days the air smelled of the sea. We were everywhere and nowhere.

We had been invited to a party that night hosted by the dean
of the college at his house in Ipswich.

I came into the room, I said, "I think we should stay home
tonight." She was standing by her desk, holding a blue envelope
in her hand, reading a letter. It had been delivered earlier that
day. Her look was intense; I mean that her attention was so focused
on what she was reading that she was unaware I had spoken. It
was impossible to discern her mood. I stood and stared at her.

All that morning Kate had been sitting at her computer. She
hadn't typed a word for nearly half an hour. I was in the living
room, reading, listening to her silence. It had been a long year for
me. For all the publicity and good reviews, my third novel had
earned me very little money. I wasn't writing; or rather, I would
begin a novel, work furiously and in high spirits on it for a month,
then drop it, utterly bored with my characters and their circum-
stances. I felt drained of energy. The heat wave had lasted nearly
a week. Kate was wearing a kimono she had bought at a Japanese
shop in London. I approached her and touched her arm and she
quickly stuffed the letter into her desk drawer. She said to me
with a look of panic: "I can't seem to get a hold on Marc's style "

"Who's the letter from?"

"It's not important."

"Everything all right?"

"I'm not going to be able to finish the translation."

"But you've almost finished."

"It's all wrong. I'll have to start over again. I'll need more time."

"Not really."

"I've missed something." Her blond hair was flecked with grey, and although I thought it attractive she hated it, she hated the idea of growing old. Her face seemed swollen with the heat, her eyes dimmed. I touched her cheek and pushed the hair away from her face.

"Has Marc come back from Paris? Why don't you call him, tell him about this?"

She turned back to her desk. "No."

"But who else can help you?"

"I just seem to be missing the focus of the story."

"I thought it was a simple detective story. A thriller. A *policier*."

"It's not, though," and when she said it her voice rose nearly to a shout.

I remembered her reading it throughout that last year, annotating the French edition with colored pencils, making notes to herself on a pad of paper. The style didn't seem especially difficult or even original. In length the sentences varied little. A man gets out of a taxi. He walks up to the entrance of a hotel.

I said, "Why don't you leave off for today." I couldn't read it in the original, but from what Kate said it seemed to me nothing more than a cheap thriller, a lurid tale of a bleaker, darker world with its own peculiar logic, its own sense of tragedy. It seemed as if Marc Rougemont and I were working the same territory.

She said, "We'll go to the party, then."

"Let's just go out together. We'll eat at a restaurant, we'll come back early. It's too hot to go up to the Linders', it's too hot to stand around a pool getting drunk with a bunch of abstract expressionists."

"I want to be with people, I want to go swimming, David, it might be my last chance before winter." She looked at me. "I just want to."

"Then we'll go down to the lake."

I sat on the edge of the bed and she turned to face me. She

was so distant. For the past six or seven months she had seemed somehow absent, as if she were only a shell, the best part of her no longer there. As though something within her had died. Lately she had said little: a silence had fallen between us, something palpable and malign, a wall that forbade emotion.

I remembered how hard we'd tried to have a baby after that visit to the Vineyard. Kate had bought a book on the subject and plotted out the fertile period of each month. What had always been the most pleasurable lovemaking became a duty, a ritual coupling, a strain for both of us. In the end we consulted doctors. Kate was perfectly capable of bearing children; I could never be a father. Her grief was something I could never completely comprehend. My grief would come later.

She shut her eyes as I touched the side of her face and drew my finger down through the shallow cleft between her breasts. Her skin was damp with perspiration. I parted her kimono and looked at her. I pressed my lips against her forehead and as I withdrew she looked in my eyes; and for a moment I grew frightened, for her look was impossible to decipher. It suddenly dawned on me that I didn't know her, not at all.

"What is it?" I said.

"I want to go swimming in Jake and Greta's pool. I'd like to go to the party. I need to get out tonight."

I rose from the bed and stood by the window. The haze of afternoon had begun to thicken; thunder was in the air, a low rumble that came suddenly upon you like a murmur in the ear. Kate slipped off her kimono. She hunted through her drawers for her bathing suit and I watched her pull it on over her pale body, slowly adjusting the garment to her shape. She took a dress from the wardrobe and put it on over her bathing suit. She placed clean panties and a towel in a canvas beach bag, then switched off the computer. I watched the words disappear. *It was nice hearing his wife's voice again.* The screen grew dark.

I said, "Maybe you should speak to your publisher about this. I'm sure they'll give you an extension."

"I don't want an extension."

"But if you're having trouble with it . . ."

And she said: "I just can't seem to get to the heart of this."

"Have you told Marc?"

And she turned to me with such a look of contempt that I had to leave the room. Now I was excluded from her world.

That evening we walked down to the lake for a swim and then changed and went for a drive. There was a restaurant in another town we liked, set on the edge of a river. You could get there by way of the back roads, passing estates and farms, riding stables, private schools. It was a quiet place; few tourists came there once summer was over. We always took a table by the window, Kate to stare at the sunlight on the water, while I was content to watch her, both of us lost in our distraction. Her heart was a mansion. Some rooms were open to me, others remained closed. I had come to respect the locked door, the unyielding latch, the sudden hush behind the wall. And then I came to fear them.

That evening was the last we ever spent together. I had seen it coming: a weakening in her smile, a look of indifference in her eyes, few words spoken. She picked at her food, only occasionally taking a sip of her wine. She merely nodded or shook her head in response to my questions. I grasped her fingers and felt the chill in them, as if the blood were withdrawing from her. Sometimes I thought of this as a curtain between us, thick and insulating, absorbent of sound and light. And then she turned to me. And I could see that love had fled.

I cheated, of course. I have no snapshot of the look. But I can't seem to forget it.

A COIN

A few minutes before midnight the phone rang. It had happened this way before.

Phone calls made by no one at all: silent phone calls, as though someone wanted to listen in on my confusion, my grief. In the days following my return from Italy they came after sunset, sometimes as late as midnight, and then, towards the end of my first week back, just before dawn. It was not an isolated series of wrong numbers, there was nothing arbitrary about them, there was no question of coincidence or accident, and it was the regularity of the calls, an apparent pattern, that began to unnerve me. I found it difficult to return to sleep. Once, as I sat up in bed, trying to catch my breath, I cried into the phone, "Kate?" and with audible ferocity the caller hung up. And then I lay awake until daybreak.

I looked up from my book. Outside a dog barked. Music quietly played on the stereo. I reached forward and switched it off. I let the phone ring twice more and then I picked it up and listened. After a few moments he began to speak.

It was Marc Rougemont, calling from New York. He sounded as if he'd been drinking. *Bon soir mon ami.*

"It's late," I said.

"Did I wake you?"

"No. It's just."

"I did wake you. I have been trying to reach you."

I had been wondering why Marc hadn't acknowledged Kate's death. The day after the funeral I had phoned their American publisher, asking her editor to pass on the message, certain it would reach him wherever he was. Yet I'd heard nothing.

I said, "You know about Kate." I saw the box, the flames.

He said, "I'm sorry, David. It was a terrible thing. What can I say?"

At a loss for words: the phrase rang in my ears. *Words cannot express.* I had received countless sympathy cards and letters laced with just such expressions. Only now did I understand. Now the clichés absorbed significance. For Marc, even for me, Kate's death existed in some other realm where words were irrelevant, where time was meaningless, where you walked a fine line between howl and silence.

I hadn't seen him in almost a year. In fact I had very little to do with Marc Rougemont, for he was Kate's business, not mine. She dealt with him only by mail or on the phone, and on the one occasion he had flown up to stay with us.

Now Marc was coming to Boston for two days. He'd been invited to give a talk at the French Library on Marlborough Street, to sign copies of the French edition of his book at Schoenhof's in Cambridge. There was a friend he wanted to visit. *Une amie,* he called her. Then he'd return to New York. For all the usual reasons he'd been thinking of settling in Manhattan: he'd been offered another contract by the university, money was available, he'd made friends. His photo began to appear in magazines, a tall good-looking man drinking champagne or stepping out of a trendy nightclub.

There were women. "There are some things one cannot resist," he said with an easy laugh. He wondered if I could join him for lunch the next day.

"I'll pick you up, if you like," I said. Marc would be staying at one of the more expensive hotels in town.

"No. We'll meet someplace else. I don't know Boston at all well. Recommend a restaurant."

"One I like or one I can't afford?"

"It doesn't matter. I'm renting a car, I'll even drive up to your place if you want."

I said, "I'd like to get out. Let me meet you at the hotel and we can make arrangements there, all right?"

The next morning I left the house two hours earlier than I'd planned. For the first time since Kate's death I actually desired to go into the city, to walk the streets and mingle with crowds and get jostled in the overheated shops. For the first time I felt my eyes were open.

A week earlier I had driven to Cambridge, where I browsed in bookstores, in record shops. It all seemed pointless to me, words on a page, notes played on a piano, it was all somehow less important now that Kate wasn't here. Even the sight of my own novels, neatly shelved or stacked on a table, left me unmoved. I felt something inexpressible locked away within myself.

I avoided conversations, I declined dinner invitations, as though to forget what I had lost even for one moment would be unforgivable. It wouldn't, it couldn't, last forever. Soon I would return to my post at the art college; soon I would be writing again; eventually I would return to life and the consolations of fiction: this is what I told myself.

Then what would happen?

Once I'd truly gotten over Kate.

Once I realized I was alone.

Then what?

Would it begin again, the shifting eyes, the frank exchanged looks, the attempts to connect, the endless witty comments; dates arranged and broken, silent expensive meals, the quick gasping clinches at midnight, the inevitable disappointments?

The day before I was to meet Marc in Boston I had driven into town to pick up a bottle of Scotch, a newspaper. I went into the little bookshop to have a fresh look at the competition. They looked out at me from their jacket photographs with their reptilian smiles, their murderous stares. On a shelf devoted to works by local authors my three volumes stood next to Updike's vast oeuvre, all rabbits and centaurs, collecting dust. A woman was leafing through an art book: paintings of women reading letters, weighing pearls and gold; familiar pictures. I looked at her, I looked into her eyes as she glanced up at me, simultaneously we smiled and then I walked out on what might have become a different story, or merely an echo of the first. And it was odd, but that glance somehow sustained me; at least until the next morning, when I woke feeling as diminished and pathetic as I had felt the day before.

I turned on the wipers and watched them sweep the drizzle off the windshield. The roads leading to the highway were deserted save for the Volvo wagons and Range Rovers toting carpools to nearby private schools, the horse trailers slowly negotiating the sharp turns. The autumn tourists had fled, the leaves had turned brown.

Though I was an hour early I stepped into the lobby of the hotel. The man at the desk said, "There's no Mr. Rougemont staying here."

"That's impossible."

"No one by that name is registered at this hotel." The man looked curiously at me, sizing me up.

I turned away and then looked at him. "Has by any chance a message been left at the desk for me? My name is Reid."

The man didn't even bother to look. I thanked him and walked off.

Perhaps his flight had been delayed. Or there was traffic out of the airport. But then of course the man behind the desk would have known the name, spotted the reservation.

Now the sun was out. I began walking, making my way through the dense lunchtime crowds.

I continued walking. I looked at the buildings on either side of the wide street, I glanced at the faces of those who passed me by. I wondered how long it would be before I made my move. It seemed impossible that I could stay on in the country, teaching and writing, living in a house that for me was haunted: by Kate, by our marriage, by whatever had compelled her to kill herself.

I thought of moving to Boston, where there were people, where voices could be heard. Where I could escape the intimacy of our past. It would be akin to shedding a previous life. As if I could ever leave it all behind: two years of marriage to Kate. That would always be with me. It was only the skin of life that I would discard: my unchanging routine at the college, at my desk; the house, the things that filled it.

I imagined myself coming back to life: going to films, concerts, museums. I thought of myself attending parties, meeting people. I remembered my mother asking when I would marry again.

But I would never marry again, because in a way I could not completely understand that act alone would destroy Kate forever.

I pictured myself growing into old age, becoming like the tiny figures in old photographs of city boulevards, bearded, immobile, propped on their sticks, out for a stroll in the afternoon sun of another era, preparing to return to an apartment lined with bookshelves, where the dust rose twice a day, where the air was full of whispers. I would live in the shell of my solitude, trying to catch glimpses of things lost in the past as they momentarily sparkled in my dark memory. I would muster the energy to walk the long galleries of museums. From the public library I would borrow forgotten novels, their pages stained with chocolate fingerprints and droplets of grease, the shabby residue of solitary meals. On long winter evenings I would listen to piano sonatas and late string quartets, the wrenching debates between violin and cello, the terrible rhythms of age and darkness. The skin on my face would take on the hue of an old tallow candle, my bones would creak.

I thought: I can forestall this. And my body shuddered, as though suddenly struck with pain. It was time for me to rejoin the living, put myself back in the picture.

I realized I had walked some distance from the hotel. The crowds had thinned out. Bars and nightclubs, one after another, each nearly identical, lined the street. Your steps went *crunchcrunch* over broken glass. People stood here and there, not idly but designedly, shifting their weight from foot to foot, eyeing the passersby, seeking eye contact, the beckoning finger.

I paused to get my bearings and then I saw Marc come out of a small hotel across the road. A sign that read Rooms Daily Weekly Monthly hung from the side of it. The hotel was above a nightclub called the Blue Hour. A neon woman danced in the darkened window, a sinister indigo shimmy from left to right, left to right.

Marc lit a cigarette and looked at his watch. He seemed agitated, impatient. A woman walked out of the hotel and joined him. She wore a short denim skirt and black leather jacket, dark glasses. Her hair was like Kate's, blond, neatly cut, thick. They walked to the end of the street and disappeared around the corner.

I realized I wasn't meant to have seen Marc and the woman. I began to follow them. The darkened side street was filled with more bars. An elderly Chinese man stood in front of a grocery and spat on the ground. The air smelled of conflict, stale things, things that had died. Loud music came from nowhere. Marc and the woman went into a bar called the Piccadilly. Strung plastic beads hung from the door frame. Someone touched my arm. She said, "I give good head, babycakes." She looked no older than fifteen. A man watched her carefully from a doorway.

I began walking back to the hotel. In thirty minutes I was supposed to meet Marc. I was five minutes early when I eventually entered the lobby. The tall man in the tweed jacket rose from his seat and took my hand.

‡   ‡   ‡

Tall and slim and fair, not small and compact and dark like me.

Kate used to say, "Marc is your opposite," and then she would laugh, because she knew I disliked characterizing people by what they were not. Perhaps I seemed so short only because Marc was that much taller, though he was exactly the same height as Kate.

That time Marc Rougemont came to visit us: standing in the living room, looking at the print over my desk, the one Kate had brought back with her from London. He looked at the woman holding the balance; and then he turned and looked at Kate before looking at me and smiling.

He had seen it too, the resemblance.

It was his first trip to America. He had been invited as guest lecturer for a year at the French department at NYU. He phoned Kate from New York a few days after he had arrived and she asked him to spend the weekend at our house. She had a number of questions about the translation, she hoped he would be willing to help her. We drove to the airport and met him at the Pan Am shuttle. On the way back they spoke French to each other, and I caught glimpses of him in the rearview mirror. He said, "Let's speak English. Your husband feels left out," and with his hand he brushed his hair away from his eyes and smiled at the back of my head.

Marc's novel was Kate's first big commission. His book had been a bestseller in France and had done well in translation in Italy, Germany, the Netherlands. A film was about to go into production in Paris and Amsterdam. *Point de fuite:* Kate was intending to call it *Vanishing Point.* Nothing he had published before had been as successful, although his reputation as someone who had adroitly combined the techniques of the *nouveau roman* with the clichés of the *policier* had steadily grown. Kate's former employer in London had bought the UK rights and Kate was signed to do the English translation. It was also due to be published in America. His was twice the success my book had been: he had the reviews and the sales. I had only the reviews.

I looked at him, a quiet man in blue jeans and white shirt and tweed jacket. He spoke fluent English. He was good-looking. He was French.

"Kate gave that to me when we were married. It used to hang in her flat in London."

He raised his eyebrows. "Now I see. Of course. It looks so much like your wife," and he turned back to it, catching a glance at her as she came into the room. "Not so much physically, you know. But in her attitude, her expression," and he shaped the words in the air with his hands.

Kate said that dinner was ready and she stood there, holding a lighted match to the wick of a candle, looking at him as he turned back to her.

‡ ‡ ‡

The restaurant Marc had chosen had been recommended to him by a friend of his in New York. I recognized it as the most expensive place in town. As I sat a woman at a nearby table looked up at me, catching my eye, suggesting a smile. Though she wasn't the woman I had seen Marc with before, she was the image of Kate and for a moment my breath was taken away.

I said to Marc, "How's your hotel? Any good? It can't be bad, considering what they must charge. I bet they even put a bonbon on your pillow at night."

"It's okay."

"I arrived a bit early. It seems you were out." I looked at him and smiled. I was about to say: *I saw you earlier,* then thought better of it. I wondered why I thought better of it. I had never before felt constrained from speaking my mind to anyone. Yet it seemed as if what I had witnessed, Marc and the blond woman coming out of a hotel, in some peculiar way hinted at Kate's death. As if one obliquely reflected some aspect of the other, the two ideas coming to me in quick successive images. Like a coin spinning its way across a table.

"I'm not staying there, actually," Marc said.

"I know that. That's why I was asking."

"My reservations were changed by the people who had invited me to talk. But it was too late to let you know."

"How long have you been in the city?"

He looked at his watch. "Actually about one hour."

Marc looked at me and vaguely smiled. I wondered why he'd invited me. He didn't seem particularly pleased about it. I had met him only once before, I barely knew him. He said, "I have to tell you that I was so very sorry to hear about Kate. I still can't believe it. It's so," and I said, "I understand."

"But why would she do such a thing?"

" 'Thing.' What thing?"

He shrugged a little, his hand trembled. "I simply assumed she had—you know . . ."

"Killed herself? Yes, she probably did."

"But why? Why would she do this?"

"I don't know," I said.

"She," and he lifted a hand slightly and looked away from me, "she never said anything before?"

"She left about two weeks earlier. She went to New York. She was going to stay at her sister's place. She said she needed time to think. It was the worst two weeks I'd ever spent in my entire life."

"Time to think," and he smiled uncertainly. "Was she troubled by something, by the work, for instance? If this happened because of my book I would."

And I interrupted: "I don't know what it was."

"She left no notes, no letter. Nothing like that?"

"No notes," I said. "Nothing."

Marc lit another cigarette and studied the menu. I had hoped we wouldn't have to discuss Kate. Now that there was no chance of ever seeing her again, of resuming our life together, all talk of her only invested her with a kind of false existence, as if she were a manifestation at a seance, ready to utter a few cryptic words, only to revert to mist and air a moment later.

I looked up, around, beyond him. I looked at the woman at the other table, the one who reminded me so much of Kate. The contrast between her black dress and her blond hair and her paleness was striking; it brought to mind an eclipse. She was talking to a man whose back was visible to me. She rested her chin on the palm of her hand, she smoked a cigarette, played with a fork, shot a quick glance at me. I watched as she lifted her wine glass, I looked at her fingers. She reminded me of the ice in my glass: brittle and angular.

I said, "I'm sorry she never finished the translation. I don't even know how much she'd done of it. She couldn't seem to grasp the style of it. I never really understood what had happened." I pressed my fingers together and looked in bewilderment at Marc. "A man gets out of a taxi, goes into a hotel."

He shrugged, he seemed distracted.

I sipped my drink. My eyes shifted an inch. I saw the man's back, hunched inelegantly, and just beyond it two blue eyes meeting mine. It was as if a door had suddenly blown open.

"I saw you earlier." There, I'd said it.

"What do you mean, earlier?"

"With some woman. You were coming out of a hotel in the Combat Zone."

He seemed amused. "Is that what they call it? Look, she was just a woman I'd picked up."

"A whore. A tart."

"Yes, of course."

"Harlot. Trollop. Wench. Doxy. You paid her."

He smiled and fingered the rim of his glass. "Naturally." It was as if he'd been shopping for a piece of fruit.

"Did you drive a hard bargain, talk her down a bit in price, ask for a bargain-basement blow job? Or was the drink you bought her afterwards part of the deal?"

He laughed. "No, no, nothing like that." He looked me in the eye. "So tell me. What are you going to do now? Stay on in your house? And you have your teaching responsibilities."

"I took a leave of absence. I'm in no shape to teach. I don't know what I'll do. I'm not ready to write anything yet, I don't have the strength to invent a plot. I still have to get my bearings." Suddenly I felt very low. Kate's death had meant nothing to him, everything to me. No one had a right to be happy when I was grieving.

A bottle of wine was produced and Marc examined the label, smelled the cork, tasted it. It seemed hardly worth the effort. In the end it all ended up in the sewers. The waiter brought our meal, and quietly, almost under his breath, he said, "Be careful, it's hot."

The blonde's escort now seemed agitated: you could tell by the way he moved his head, this way and that, up and down, as if trying to drive home a point. The woman also looked angry, she clenched her fist and then splayed her fingers, she said, "I would never do such a thing," and then the man said something inaudible to her. She said, "No more fucking ultimatums," and she turned away from him, pressing her lips together, catching my glance en route.

I watched as the couple rose from their table. The man turned briefly to me, caught my eye and walked off as the woman looked inside her handbag and then slung it over her shoulder. This time she avoided my look and stared instead at the back of Marc's head.

He said: "Perhaps you should move. Travel for a bit. Get your mind off things, go back to New York."

I laughed.

"Look, why not New York?" Marc held his hands apart. "Kate once told me she'd always wanted to live there. At least whenever she was there she said it."

I looked at him. "She never told me that."

I let him go on.

"Sometimes I'd run into her in the city. Once at my publisher's office. More than once, actually."

Kate had never mentioned it.

I waited.

"She seemed to like New York. That's all I'm trying to say."

"She died there."

"I know that," said Marc. "I'm sorry, I shouldn't have said anything. Forget it."

For a few minutes we ate in silence. Had he invited me because he felt guilty for his silence over Kate's death? I seemed to be missing the point of it all.

Through the smoked glass of the restaurant windows I watched the crowds walk by. I saw the woman who had been sitting at the next table. She was standing, her back to me. The man left

the restaurant and came up to her and raised his hand in the air
and she flinched and walked away. No one seemed to notice it.

Marc said, "Look. If you like you can come and stay with me
in the city for a week or two. It will do you good."

"That's nice of you."

"After all."

"You don't need to say this."

"I mean, Kate was my."

"You don't owe me anything." I said it a bit too loudly, and
turning his face slightly sideways he stared at me. Then he checked
his watch. "My God, I have to be at my talk in twenty minutes."
He lifted a hand and caught hold of the waiter's sleeve and asked
for the bill. He pulled a credit card from his wallet and handed
it to the young man.

When we got outside Marc began walking rapidly away from
the restaurant. He said, "I told you I rented a car. I was lucky, I
found a space just around the corner." He came to a sudden halt
and took a key from his pocket. He inserted it in the lock of a
pale blue Mercedes. A parking ticket flapped under a wiper blade.
He took it and tore it into pieces and let them flutter into the
breeze. Without looking at me he said, "Can I drop you off on
the way?"

I looked at the car. I looked at Marc. I ran out of words.

THE RIVER

It seemed pointless to return home so early. The day had grown bright and warm. To return home meant the house, the fallen leaves, the familiar smells, the memories. Soon it would be winter, meaning long solitary days as the snow gathered into tall drifts. Meaning the endless nights alone. Then she would come to life for me, my wife, standing in the living room; lying beside me on the bed. Smiling at me as we walked to Covent Garden, breaking the silence with her lovely rich laugh. And then she would disappear; and for the hundredth time die.

I stopped and bought a newspaper and turned to the film listings, then read the front page. An artist from the Netherlands had been found dead in a Boston hotel room the night before, an apparent suicide. Twenty years earlier he had been a celebrity. Since then his career had come to a standstill. For a while he lived rough on the streets of Amsterdam, he took on odd jobs, he moved unrecognized through a society that had once flocked to his shows, read his name in textbooks. Once he had been quite a ladies' man, you'd see him in magazines and newspapers, dining with some actress or model, a cigarette between his lips, his eyes dazzled by the flash of a photographer's light. No one knew why he had come to Boston, no letter had been found: only his passport and a small suitcase. He had stepped out of the world into some tenebrous, more terrifying place where there is no room for art.

I looked at my watch and walked to the cinema, one of three located in a building not far from the hotel. The theatres themselves were small and anonymous; the seats uncomfortable, with plastic arm rests that stuck to the skin on your hands. The air smelled of stale popcorn and spilled soda. I sat in the twilight and ate nonpareils from a giant-size box. There were only six or seven other people there. Pointlessly and anxiously they stared at the blank screen. Banal music played from huge speakers. I shut my eyes for a moment. I remembered the night the Mercedes followed me, taunted me; I remembered the phone calls and I thought of Marc. Marc, who wrote of a man walking into a hotel. Who plunged a city into heat wave. Who let night fall, and then midnight; who made time pass as another watched from a darkened window.

And when I thought of Marc I thought of Kate, standing there that first time he came, watching him as she lit the candle. This is the still center of suspicion.

The lights began to dim and the blond woman from the restaurant walked in and after hesitating for a moment sat in the aisle seat directly ahead of mine. Now the film was starting.

An empty room. An empty chair. A grey morning. Something has happened.

Although it was forbidden the blond woman lit a cigarette, and with my eyes I followed the smoke as it rose above her head and uncurled in the hazy light. The film was about a woman whose husband disappears. The couple has moved to the city and one day he fails to return from work. Was he having an affair? Had

he run off to Tahiti? Would he be found floating in the river, a
pale bloated body riddled with holes? Mysteries give rise to mysteries, to the hell of uncertainty. I remembered reading the novel
on which the film was based. I remembered being simultaneously
gripped and annoyed by it, I disliked the style of the author, so
many endless sentences, so many commas. I rubbed my eyes and
tried to look at my watch when the woman on the screen suddenly
sat up in bed and pulled open her curtain and daylight flooded
the room and the music that had begun with the credits stopped.
I had been sitting there for about ten minutes. Now the woman
was speaking to a detective. As though he were addressing a child
the detective said, "Add one and one and see what you get." Now
there was a commotion going on.

The man was leaning over the blond woman. I looked up at
him. The man ignored me, or simply wasn't aware I was sitting
there. The man was stocky, solidly built, the kind of man accustomed to putting his weight behind his impulses, his desires. He
said quietly to the woman, "Get out of here."

The woman said nothing. The man took hold of her arm. He
said, "You bitch," and still the woman said nothing while I watched
impassively, frozen by the reality of it.

The man lifted his hand in the air and struck the woman across
the face with such force that she fell from her seat and sprawled
to the ground. Yet it all happened with so little noise that the
others in the cinema failed to notice. In a whisper I said, "Get
out." The man looked at me with wide eyes, as if I had suddenly
appeared out of nowhere. I stood, I said, "Leave her alone and
get out." The man looked at me for what seemed a long while. I
wondered if he carried a gun, if he was now going to relieve me
of my life.

The man looked down at the woman. Together we watched
her. She was kneeling on the floor, touching the side of her face.

Her cigarette rolled towards her hand and I snuffed it out with my toe. The man said nothing and walked away.

I reached down and helped the woman to her feet. She brushed dirt from her knees with her fingers. A large hole appeared in one of her stockings. The woman on the screen said, "I can't be certain of anything, Inspector. I just want you to help me find my husband."

I said, "Are you all right?" and my nonpareils spilled from the box onto the floor.

"Of course I'm not."

"Do you want to leave?"

"It's a lousy film, anyway."

Together we looked at the screen. A woman was walking along a rain-drenched street. It was night. The man watching her from a hotel window pulled the curtains shut and turned away.

We squinted as the bright sunlight blazed through the glass doors of the lobby. The side of the woman's face was beginning to swell. I touched it with the tips of my fingers. "Try something cold on it. An ice pack."

"I'd rather have a drink."

I looked at her. I said, "I saw you in the restaurant."

"I know."

"It's funny."

"I know."

We went into the bar of a nearby hotel. She ordered a martini. "One day he's going to kill me," she said. She tugged the olive from its little plastic saber with her teeth.

"Perhaps you should contact the," and she interrupted: "The police wouldn't be able to stop him. He's friends with all of them."

"He's a cop?"

She said nothing.

"Are you married to him?"

She said nothing. She lit a cigarette. She said that she lived in Boston, that she wasn't often here as she traveled a great deal in her line of work. She said, "I work for a bank," and then turned away and examined her face carefully in the mirror of her compact. She raised her fingers and ran them gently over the swelling and then suddenly turned and looked at me.

She said, "You're married," and with her eyes indicated the ring on my finger.

I explained simply and emotionlessly what had happened. It seemed pointless to draw a stranger into it, the darkness of the past few months. I watched as she listened to me, I looked at her eyes, her mouth, measuring her reactions, and then she said, "This is a terrible thing. Horrible. I don't even know your name and yet I'm sorry. I am, really."

I lifted the side of my glass to her face and she pressed herself against it, letting the cold soothe her. She shut her eyes and smiled and then I sipped from my glass and set it down. I said, "This man who struck you. Is he one of your clients?"

"That was a personal matter."

"What's your name?"

"And yours?"

I told her and she looked at me, as if to see whether face and name coincided. I wrote my name and phone number on a paper napkin.

It grew dark. Night was falling. We walked and watched as a solitary police boat plied the Charles, cutting slowly through it, a searchlight sweeping the dark patches beneath the bridges. A few people stood watching, anticipating. Joggers passed by on the narrow footpath, panting, their breaths visible in the cold air. The river slapped against its banks, smelled faintly of decay, snatched at moonlight. I looked at the woman and for a single moment Kate stepped back into my life.

‡   ‡   ‡

Her name was Denise Casterman.

Before this I had never liked the name Denise. Denise: a teenager in a cheerleader's skirt, forever sweet sixteen.

Denise Casterman. Denise. Now it acquired a certain richness. I thought of her thick hair, her icy blue eyes, the warmth of her hand in mine when she said goodbye. Her voice, a husky whisper, the voice of nightfall, of words exchanged across a pillow, the voice of risk.

I wondered whether I would ever hear from her. I wondered if she had bothered to save my phone number. She hadn't given me hers, she said she was often out of town. I wondered if she even remembered me. I felt as if I had lost something valuable. Over and over in my mind I saw her: talking to the man in the restaurant; at the cinema, being struck to the ground, in pain. Afterwards, in the half-light of the hotel bar, sipping a martini, her face bruised. In the inky reflection off the water as we walked along the river.

I told her about Kate. I spoke of my work as a writer. She marveled at my patience. "I could never do that," she said. "It must be difficult keeping yourself sane," and I laughed, for Kate had once said the same thing to me. *Just the idea of it,* she said at the restaurant in Covent Garden, that first week I was in London. *How splendid to spend your hours and days in a complete fiction. Just to get away from things, to get into the lives of others.*

But they're not real, I told her.

I know, she said with pleasure, that smile of hers, that lovely enigmatic grin, her eyes half-closed, blossoming in my memory as the juggler's last Indian club fell to the ground.

Then it came to me: our last night together, the night before she left for New York. I was sitting on the edge of the bed. She shut her eyes. I touched the side of her face. I pressed my lips against her forehead and as we separated Kate's expression, impenetrable, alien, banished me forever from her world.

These were the bookends of the life we had shared.

I stopped and lightly rested my fingers on her arm, and gently she pulled away from me. We crossed the bridge into Back Bay. I said to Denise, "You followed me today, didn't you. You followed me into the cinema."

"I happened to see you go in. I was frightened, I thought you might help me."

"You'd also seen me in the restaurant."

She looked at me.

I said, "That man threatened you, didn't he."

She smiled. She said, "Thank you for the drink. Thank you also for being so kind. I have an early flight tomorrow," and she lifted her hand and stopped a taxi.

We had walked for nearly an hour. I knew how the mind worked. I knew that next time, if there was a next time, I would see her differently. Now I imagined a woman slightly taller than myself, with ash-blond hair and blue eyes. Yet because she was too recently placed in my memory I couldn't recall her expressions, the nuances of her. I thought of Kate, how throughout our two years of marriage she changed constantly, and I thought this is what being human is about, what love also must consist of, this continual renewal of another person.

Denise Casterman.

Denise.

Four days had passed.

She had said little about herself, only that she was a trust officer, working on behalf of clients who required a more individual service.

Married?

Separated.

Often in Boston?

Once a week. Sometimes twice. Sometimes more.

I thought of the restaurant, how she came into view beyond Marc's shoulder. She sat in front of me in the cinema. We had a drink, took a walk. A series of accidents, quick glances, crossed paths.

A net. A web.

I thought of the Mercedes following me, driving me off the highway. One idea led to another.

It's the details, isn't it, that begin to get to you.

I wasn't quite sure when it occurred to me, the idea that Marc had been somehow involved with Kate. No, that's not true. I could see precisely when it came into my mind, I could actually establish it, as if it were a point on a map, definable by coordinates of degree and minute. Possibly it had always been there, simmering just below the surface, waiting for words to establish its identity. That first night he came to stay with us: somehow I had registered the origins of it then, in the way their looks crossed, the way their attentions froze, one upon the other as Kate lighted the candle: as though I had suddenly turned my eyes towards the future and were meeting my own at this moment of recognition.

Paris was lovely.

Perhaps my suspicion was merely an illusion produced by hindsight, and as I thought about this I realized there was nothing to it, it was an irrational way of measuring things. It was a fiction devised by me to fill the spaces, because part of my mind was always spinning plots, turning over lines of dialogue, seeking form and structure. Yet I could feel betrayal deep within my body, like a physiological reaction: a nudge of certainty, of dread.

And though I couldn't prove that the car following me so closely had been Marc's, or the phone calls had come from him, they remained a kind of intimation, like repeated images in a novel insinuating themselves into the mind of the reader, pointing towards some greater truth.

And then in one breath Marc had mentioned Kate and New

York, and the mosaic seemed complete. *Sometimes I'd run into her in the city. Sometimes I'd run into her.*

Just sometimes.

Consider it. In the stillness of the afternoon, as I was writing or lecturing at the college or reading, Kate and Marc may have been elsewhere, together, beyond the margins of my knowledge. Now that I was able to imagine it, to visualize the simple outlines of the scene, it achieved a reality independent of me, as if it were a work of art or a chemical reaction, a ticking bomb left in a railway terminal.

I turned the page. A woman in a painting is being urged to drink a glass of wine by a sinister smiling robust man. A second man sits at the table, seemingly oblivious to this decisive moment, his face turned away. Something terrible is about to happen. Possibly the early stages of an assault are in progress. The red ribbons in her hair appear limp and tawdry. Under his breath the man is perhaps saying, *Just another. Have one more. Enjoy yourself.* The woman's face glows with giddiness and terror and then I shut the book, for the woman's expression was too much to bear, her black beseeching eyes fixing me from a room in Delft, three hundred years earlier.

THE DETAILS

It's the details, isn't it, that begin to get to you.

It all begins between the sheets. Of a hotel room bed. Of someone else's. Of your own. One thing leads to another and so begins the Age of Analysis: every suspicion becoming an image ripe for deconstruction. A room, some room, his room, my room, another's room. The grey thickness of a summer afternoon. Somewhere a fly buzzes, a web trembles in the breeze.

She climbs the stairs.

No: they're already inside. Inside five seconds and already she can't keep her hands off him.

Now let's shift our gaze. On an armchair her clothes: dress, panties. His are scattered across the floor, trousers with legs splayed, a half-unbuttoned white shirt. Her sandals lie one atop the other by the side of the bed. The haste of it all.

The telephone receiver placed beside the telephone while a small voice says *Hello can I help you?* before the line goes cold. Do Not Disturb dangles from the doorknob.

Ne pas déranger.

Resist looking at the bed, plug your ears to the noise, the rough-and-tumble of illicit pleasure, the moans, the whispers, the sudden intake of breath.

Look: a mist of sunlight settling on the floor, the wall.

Listen: the uproar and mayhem of the city filtering through the window.

Imagine your wife in the arms of another. Watch as they ascend the stairway, see how she puts her hands on him, how intimately she touches his body, how irresistible he is to her. See the buttons slip from their holes. Listen to her words: *Oh my darling, oh yes oh yes.*

Time weighs heavily on this pair, time governs their separate existence, it presses them to the wall, it turns life into *lie.*

This is what it's like to be someone else, the Other Man.

How long had it been going on?

What is he thinking? More importantly, what is *she* thinking?

Let's go back into the room. Apply your shoulder to the door. Turn and look, force yourself: see her in his arms, listen to her words. *I love it when you do that. I love you.*

Enough.

The heart can bear just so much.

THE DREAM

Funny how we get to roam about this house at will, without quite being seen. We watch a woman weighing, a procuress anticipating her coin; a woman at her music, turning to stare because we have disturbed her with our ghostly footsteps.

Naturally we don't see any women undressing or washing. That's the sort of thing they do down in the sunny side of France: ecstatic nudes in a red and blue nightmare; women bathing, their backs lusciously curved; a naked lady at a picnic, languidly waiting for a chill.

Yet there's something altogether more intimate about these pictures, the woman with the scales, the woman putting on her necklace.

Our heroine, possibly due to a surfeit of drink, has fallen asleep at a table covered with an ornate rug on which sits a bowl of fruit and, in the foreground, a jug, presumably of wine. A glass, three-quarters empty, stands before her.

She has drunk herself into a stupor; oblivion is hers, this young woman whose portrait hangs in the Met. Her head is supported by her left hand, while her right hand, the fingers slightly curled, rests on the table. Scholars tell us this is an emblematic painting: her pose could indicate Sloth, meaning she has been drinking instead of doing something more constructive; or it could signify Melancholy, meaning she wishes to forget. For just this once.

Hanging on the wall behind her is a painting, of which we are privy to only a fragment, a figure standing beside a mask. Apparently this was a well-known emblem entitled *Love Requyres Sinceritie*. Perhaps now we know what's on the woman's mind. Someone's being deceived; someone's deceiving.

Let's say: she had received a letter. Bad news. The affair is over. *I'm tired of sneaking about,* he wrote. *I fear your husband will find us out.*

What a coward, she thinks, and suddenly she feels the old ache, the ache for him who lurks, who fears, who had once unconditionally desired this complex and alluring woman.

Let's say she'd received a letter. Good news! Now he's free; now he wants her to leave her husband, come run away with him. We saw her knuckles whiten as she read it through a second, a third time. Now she will have a drink, consider all the implications. She will do some weighing. She pours herself a glass of wine. She can't decide: stay or leave? If she stays she is sure of one thing: her husband's love. She can see it in his face as he watches her move about a room, she can feel it when she's out of his sight.

The eyes; always the eyes.

If she leaves she has before her nights of passion, like a comet blazing across the unchanging routine of her life. Then there would be no more sneaking, no more hiding, no more deceiving. The era of rendezvous and signal will have passed.

Until his eye has alighted on another; until he has grown bored with her; until he drops her. And for a moment she can see a red jacket receding, becoming a point on the horizon. Disappearing forever.

And then?

She weighs, she drinks, she considers.

She sleeps. Somewhere a fly buzzes, unnoticed by her.

Her tears dry and from the expression on her face we're reminded of a child asleep, intently serious about her rest, as though involved in a multilayered dream about a complex and difficult world, a world that overwhelms.

The light as it falls on the woman: it isn't the light of day, aslant through a window. It's more like the glow of a hundred candles, or a fire blazing in the hearth. No windows are open. No doors reveal the pathway leading to the streets that lead to the canals, to the river Schie. This is claustrophobia. Here is fever. Now there is no escape.

Which leads to what else we see: an open doorway and part of another room, bathed in a rancid yellow. But this painting by Vermeer has been x-rayed. Once a dog stood in the doorway, a little spaniel, signifying fidelity; there is even a hint that a man lingered in the other room. Now they are both gone, banished from this more ambiguous world.

Perhaps the artist wishes us to consider the possibility that the woman is dreaming about this other room. The woman, who in the long afternoon has had one too many glasses of wine, is now caught up in a dream of many dimensions, many rooms, an intricate fragile palace of tidy little connections, causes and effects, hidden stairways and dark alcoves, rooms that lead to rooms that lead to rooms. A room, some room, his room, my room, another's room. Haunted rooms, rooms that contain his scent, the echo of his footsteps, the reflection of his eyes. His words float there, secret whispers and urgings, sighs and moans. There are silent rooms, too, rooms without views, locked rooms. Eventually you return to the beginning; eventually you run out of doors and steps and hallways.

Perhaps now she will wake up.

K

It's in the book Kate had given me about a month before she left, a tall slim volume published by Abrams. This is not the weighty catalogue raisonné of a Rembrandt or Picasso that sits gathering dust on your coffee table. Vermeer left comparatively few paintings: maybe thirty-five. This book is slender, it can be taken anywhere, up and down the stairs, from one room to another.

She had left it on my desk when she came back from Boston one day, she'd taken it out of its bag, placed it down and smiled at me. It was already inscribed: *To my sweet David, with love from K.*

And then she gently kissed me on the top of my head.

"My sweet David."

Wasn't there something telling in those three words, something stiff and peculiarly formal: is this how a wife of two years conducts matters of the heart with her husband? Never before had I been *My sweet David.* I'd been *Darling* and *Love* and once or twice *You Bastard,* and for much of the time I had no name at all. I was the object of her glances, her deeper looks. I was silently included in her conversation, as if I were overhearing her private thoughts. I was a shoulder she draped her arm across. I was the person who made her laugh and sometimes cry; and sometimes she pressed her head back against the pillow and, shutting her eyes, gasped with pleasure because I was holding and loving her, because this was also something we shared. I was a presence in her life, apart yet somehow intimately connected to her. And she writes *My sweet David.*

And what did she call *him?* Some things are unimaginable, and I turn away my face from the harsh light of this knowledge.

What did she say?

Go on.

What?

The details. Always the Details.

Oh my darling, oh yes oh yes, I love it when you do that, my darling, my lover.

There. It's done.

But *My sweet David?* A definite retreat. She was playing for time. And her smile was different; it was a smile tempered by something darker than happiness, something momentous.

Possibly she knew she would go to New York, step in front of a subway train, leave me with nothing but doubts and suspicions and a volume of paintings of women reading letters, dreaming dreams, holding a balance. As though each of these contained some message for me, some individual clue to her life and death. Something lasting. As if she were saying: *Now you will come to know me.*

Now I began to read everything, every memory was placed upon the anatomist's table. I slid my scalpel down along the center of the breastbone to the pubis, heart to crotch; I peeled back the flesh from the ribcage, I broke the bones and plunged my hands into the cavity, I began my search, I bloodied my hands and like a coroner sought out traces of the crime.

I thought of Kate in another's bed. I imagined the two of them in New York, in a restaurant, strolling down Madison Avenue or sitting in a theatre, watching an opera, a ballet. The other became a pronoun: *he; him.*

I began to twist and deform her to fit the mold I had created for her. Nothing she said or did could escape it; now I would never let her go. I began to delve into the mystery of my wife, and I felt oddly uplifted, as if I had deciphered a panel of faded hieroglyphs or decoded some critical wartime wireless transmission. As if I had fallen upon some lost city of her soul, hitherto unvisited by me. Now it was in ruins, crushed below layers of ramparts, forgotten beneath the structures of conquest.

I thought of Kate that last night we had been together, how childlike she was, how vulnerable and lost. And then I thought of her lover, drawn to the light.

The glass chimney was buffed so clean that at first glance you could only discern a thin brittle outline surrounding the flame. In the faint lamplight the bowl of fruit beside it seemed drained of color; the apples and grapes we had bought at a nearby farm stand became a series of variations on the sphere. The light cast a yellow glow on Kate's face.

It was September, just after we had flown in from London. Kate hadn't been to the States before, not even to visit her sister. I watched her walking about my little rented house that first evening, touching things, smoothing her hand along the sheets on the bed, feeling the bricks of the fireplace, learning the dimensions of our home. She opened the fridge and smiled because it was as empty as hers had been that first time I'd come to her flat. Outside the wetlands produced a thick curtain of sound, hums and clicks and little rhythms, and she stood by the window, listening.

"Have we got any neighbors?" she asked, looking at me.

"You can't see them. You can barely hear them." And I was delighted, because she had said *we,* she had begun to link us together, to create a third identity. "But they're there," I added, "sitting on their front porches, shotguns in hand, waiting to catch a glimpse of us."

"Not really."

"Not really."

I lit the hurricane lamp and switched off the lights, and though it was only eight in the evening, for us it was one in the morning and we were past sleep. We sat and drank whisky and afterwards lay in each other's arms and listened to the rain fall; rain that would last for three bleak days. I said to her: "Just like home, eh?"

And she smiled.

My job at the art college had begun the previous spring; classes resumed for the year a week after we flew in from London. Kate had come to the States not only with a commission to translate Marc's novel but also with a number of steadier translating jobs she had arranged for herself in London. With my third novel just out I was in no rush to sit down to my fourth. The paperback auction had earned me enough money to buy some time for myself. I began to churn out short stories. There were books to be reviewed.

We worked in separate rooms, though if I tilted my chair back a few inches I could catch sight of her through the doorway, sitting at her desk, her hands curved over the keyboard, her chin lifted, her lips barely separated: a look of intense concentration, of focus, another aspect to Kate. I would watch her until she became aware of me and she would smile and sometimes wink before returning to her work.

In the mornings I woke early, usually around dawn, and as the light filled the room I would lie in bed and read and then put my book down and watch Kate sleep. For even then, her hair pasted to her cheek, her expression unguarded and childlike, she struck me as unerringly beautiful. And she would wake and smile and pull me towards her.

And yet there was something inscrutable about my wife. She seemed to lack any desire for intimacy; as though were she to come too close to me she might burn herself, be consumed. She would grow abstracted and quiet, as distant and guarded as she had been those first moments we met in London: and I would be left only with the sound of my own voice echoing in a deserted room.

What is it?

Nothing.

Tell me.

And she would shake her head and walk off.

Perhaps it was her previous affair that had wounded her; perhaps she simply no longer trusted others. Possibly she had lost all faith in herself.

Occasionally while I was working I would see her outside the house, walking in her green Wellington boots and oilskin jacket, inspecting what she called "our garden," avoiding the vast, intricate spiderwebs that linked shrub to tree, tree to house, invisible unless the sun struck them just so; and it was at such times that I sensed a precariousness to our marriage, as if Kate were at the end of a string held by me that might at any moment snap free. I began to watch her as one does a patient during a serious illness, anticipating crisis, hoping for recovery. At such times she was unreachable, unapproachable, unaware of me; as though she had somehow escaped me.

I watched as her eyes followed the erratic flight of a yellow butterfly, as it alighted on a leaf, on the grass, as it floated away on the crest of a breeze, leaving her alone surrounded by webs, standing in the dense uncut grass of early autumn.

These moods began to deepen. She grew unhappy with life in

the States. She missed the city, the buses, the tube trains, the pubs. Even the things she most complained of when we lived in London became treasured memories to her, the dog shit on the pavements, the stink of refried beef fat at the fish-and-chip shop. She missed her friends, she missed reading *The Independent* over toast and marmalade every morning. She missed the theatre and the "News at Ten" on Channel 4 and the chicken vol-au-vent from the Rosslyn Deli in Hampstead. The little details of her life there: they got to her very quickly.

A month passed, and she was saying: "It's too quiet here."

"That's right."

"How can you stand it?"

"Anything is better after New York."

"You're just saying that because your marriage went bad."

"It didn't go bad. It was rotten from the start."

"Piss off."

She grew sullen, she began to withdraw. She complained about inferior American bacon, the newspapers, the endomorphs who endlessly wandered the shopping malls; she railed against Massachusetts drivers, medical waste washed up on North Shore beaches. The man who hosted the morning classical-music program on public radio drove her to distraction with his interminable pauses. She made long phone calls to friends back in England, former colleagues, college chums. Phone calls in which minutiae were touched upon: the weather at that precise moment in London; who was working, and where; the headline in that day's *Evening Standard*.

I took the phone from her and replaced it.

"What the hell are you doing, David?"

"This is costing us a fortune."

"Right." She got up and went into the bedroom and, banging them noisily against the walls and floor, took down her suitcases from the shelf in the closet.

I stood and watched her. "Going out then, are you?" I enjoyed imitating her accent, copying her expressions.

She said nothing.

"I'll miss you."

"Good," she said. "Good good good."

Normally so careful with her clothes, she now bunched them into balls and stuffed them in her cases. I continued to watch her. Part of me was terrified she would leave and never return. If I took my eyes off her she would disappear, steal away.

"You know," I said, and she continued to ignore me. "You know. Listen. Listen, Kate. Look."

"Don't say you're sorry, damn you."

"You took the words right out of my mouth."

"And you think your being sorry will make it all better?"

"It's worth a try, isn't it?"

"Glib bastard." She took the photo of her parents from the shelf and laid it carefully in the suitcase, between the folds of a sweater. "I hate you. I hate everything about you. Now I'm finished packing." And she sat on the bed, the cases still open, clothes tumbling out of them.

"Can you tell me where you're going?"

"Home."

"Home. What home?"

"Just home, damn you."

"But this is your home. Our home. You haven't got a home in England anymore."

Now the tears came. I sat beside her on the bed and held her face between my hands. "I know," I said. "I know."

"You don't know."

"You're right, I don't know. Are you really miserable here?"

"It's just so bloody different. I can't get used to it."

"You've got work to do. That novel to translate."

She turned away from me. She said nothing.

Then: "He's coming, you know. Marc Rougemont."

She had said it so quietly I seemed to miss it.

"Marc Rougemont's coming."

"To the States?"

And she nodded. "I want to see him. I have to meet him."

I can still see her standing there, absolutely still, holding a lighted match to the wick of a candle, looking at him as he turned back to look at her.

‡ ‡ ‡

And so I began to speculate. I wondered what had pushed her, what had compelled her to kill herself.

As though it were a work of the imagination, something devised and executed by an artist, Kate's death seemed utterly beyond me, a vast abstract mystery existing simultaneously on different levels. Something you accept and don't question. Something you walk away from; that in the long perspective of time grows smaller, flees the mind.

A woman stands on a platform in a New York subway station. A train approaches, the woman disappears.

A man stands by a window in his hotel room, guardedly watching the dubious charade of other lives. He picks up the phone.

I dialed the number.

When Josie answered I said at once, "Kate was staying with you before she died. Tell me everything."

"David?"

"Yes."

"I told you all I know."

"You've left something out. An element is missing, a piece of the puzzle, something small, something you've overlooked. The night before she left Boston she wasn't herself, she was a stranger to me. She'd been like that before, but this was the worst I'd seen her. I have to know everything."

Like a pain that throbs it came to me again: *he* was in New York the same time as Kate.

"She did act rather oddly," Josie said. "She didn't seem very well. She looked pale. She had very little appetite. She vomited once or twice during the time she was here, she said it was nothing. So I forgot about it."

"When she arrived in New York," I began, "when you saw her at the airport, did she say anything?"

"I didn't meet her there."

What?

"She came to the apartment."

"Directly to the apartment?"

"Of course."

"But she told me you were supposed to meet her."

"She rang me a few days earlier. She said she'd prefer to come on her own."

I stared at the top of her desk. For some reason I slid open her drawer and began sifting through what was left there, pads of paper, rubber bands, pencils, paper clips, things. I tried to remember, I said, "She took the six o'clock shuttle."

"She said there'd been a delay. She didn't get here until eleven."

She'd walked off the plane into some pocket of timelessness. It was a ridiculous notion. Ideas flooded my head. I said, "And how did she seem?"

"Tired."

"Did she explain the delay?"

"What's this all about, David?"

"Answer me."

"The delay?"

"Did she explain?"

"Just a delay."

I thought of Kate calmly stepping off the subway platform without a second thought.

"And when she was staying with you, did she ever leave, go for a walk, that sort of thing?" I asked.

"Yes, sometimes. A great many times, actually."

"For a long time, for hours?"

Josie let out a brief laugh. "I suppose so."

"And she always returned, she never spent the night out?"

Again Josie laughed. "Of course she returned. I mean, how absurd, David. If anything was going on in her life it wasn't happening while she was staying with us."

I could see it all now. Now I could visualize the entire matter, not as if it were a work of fiction, to be pursued from one page to the next, but as a painting on a wall: with every detail visible all at once. It seemed to say to me: *Take it all in.*

Kate had looked pale, she had been ill.

He came often to New York.

I'd occasionally run into her, he told me.

I thought of her in bed with him. Little trysts, quick clinches taking place at odd moments, a free quarter-of-an-hour before she had to tidy herself and return to Josie's with tales of trips to museums, masterpieces glimpsed, the inevitable Rembrandt, the rare Vermeer. I imagined Marc between my wife's legs and wondered what was going through her mind, whether she felt pleasure or pain or guilt or disgust. Or simply nothing at all.

A web; a fly.

Bzz.

She looked pale. She had very little appetite.

I remembered the day the results of my fertility test came in, how disappointed we both were, how suddenly dispirited Kate was, and I held her in my arms for what seemed like hours as she moved into a darkness beyond tears.

But something had changed. Something was growing within her. She'd had an affair, become pregnant, and killed herself because the symmetry of her life had gone awry.

This is what my mind was formulating.

That night I dreamed I was sitting with Kate in a flat that belonged to us and yet was unknown to me, in a city that resembled both London and New York and that could also be called Paris, perhaps because my novels were always set in this hybrid metropolis of my imagination with its maze of subterranean tunnels, networks of elevated trains, bridges over a serpentine river. At night shadows merged and strangers stepped out of darkened doorways, people disappeared, others went mad.

We were sitting together on a sofa facing a mantelpiece, the large windows behind us casting a pale wintry light. I was next to Kate and yet because I was looking straight ahead, at the fading light reflecting off the large mirror over the mantel, I could not see her. She existed rather as a sensation, the way one feels the heat of the sun, the onset of headache. She said, "Please help me, I think someone's trying to hurt me," and when I found I couldn't turn to her I said, "I can't, you'll have to see for yourself, look in the mirror."

"Someone is trying to choke me."

There was a door far to the left of the mantelpiece, at the end of the room. There was a loud knock and it swung violently open and before I could see who was entering I awoke to the sound of the phone ringing, feeling as if I had just escaped a violent death.

It was Denise Casterman. "I'll be in Boston again in a few days. Can we meet? Same place, the hotel bar, say at four on Friday? I must," she said, "I'd like to see you again."

"Say it again."

"I woke you."

"Say it again."

"I'd like to see you, David."

"And the rest. Say it."

I wrote it down. And when I was fully awake a minute later I looked at it.

4:00 hotel bar
Meet K.

GIRL
INTERRUPTED
AT HER MUSIC

A man gets out of a taxi, goes into a hotel.

The city was in the grip of a heatwave.
Night fell. Midnight arrived.
Time passed.

He stood in his room and poured himself another drink. It
was a warm evening and he unbuttoned his shirt. He put down
his glass and switched off the lamp and parted the curtains.
A man and a woman entered a room in the building across the
road. The light seemed bright. It was nearly half past one
in the morning. The woman removed her coat and tossed it
over the back of a chair. The man lit a cigarette and glanced
out the window. He looked into the street, checked his watch,
drew his fingertips once across his forehead. The woman was
wearing a blue dress. She began speaking to the man, her mouth
stretched taut in anger. The man slowly turned, took a few
steps forward and slapped the woman, propelling her backwards

*against a wall, her hair whirling as she spiraled through the
air. The man watching them picked up the phone.*

*The man and the woman both suddenly stopped. She put
her hand to her head and lifted the receiver to her ear. The
man in the hotel room said only, "I'm back," and then
hung up.*

It was nice hearing his wife's voice again.

Wait.

It was nice hearing his wife's voice again.

That's all there was: the first page.

I phoned Kate's publisher in New York: they'd received nothing
from her beyond occasional assurances that her work was pro-
gressing, that things were moving along. Now the project had been
assigned to another translator.

I began to search the files of Kate's computer and turned up
nothing. Her copy of Marc's book was filled with notes and un-
derlinings and arrows. She had read the book once, twice, possibly
three times. Yet all she'd completed was the first page.

With my year of high-school French I could make nothing of
his novel, I could decipher only the *bonjours*, the *je t'aimes*, the
adieus. I looked at her marks in it, the blue ones, the red ones,
each used as part of her system of annotation.

A man stood at a window and watched his wife and another
man in a room.

Kate must have known what was going to happen. Yet she
seemed to be afraid to turn his novel into her words. Because she
felt compromised by it? Because the truth would somehow emerge
from the sentences and paragraphs of his story, as though slipping
free from the knots and cords of a net?

Because she felt trapped within the fiction?

Because she simply felt trapped?

A hotel room. Think of it.

Ne pas déranger.

I love it when you do that. I love you.

I put the book down and lifted the telephone receiver and dialed the number. The phone was answered after the sixth ring: I actually counted them. Marc sounded vaguely annoyed. Then he recognized my voice and laughed. He said he'd been eating breakfast and reading his mail.

"At half past eleven in the morning?" And he laughed.

I considered the two of us holding the phones in our hands, the distance between us, and in my mind's eye I saw Kate that last day of our life together. That look of hers. The heat of the afternoon. The moment I realized I'd become a stranger to my wife. I again saw the blue envelope, and a sequence of events took shape in my mind that led me to picture Marc on the other end of the line; just as whatever the envelope had contained had drawn her to him.

"I was up late last night," he said. "I was at a party. So you've decided to come to New York after all."

After a moment I said, "I can't get away. Not now. Look, Marc, I must."

And impatiently Marc said: "Yes yes, go on."

"I must know if you'd seen Kate recently. I mean just before her death."

"How could I have done that?"

"You said you often ran into her in New York."

"Only occasionally. We'd just run into each other, on the street, in a restaurant. That's all."

"In Boston as well?"

There was a pause.

"Once or twice. When I came up to see a friend I'd sometimes speak to her."

"To Kate."

"Yes, to Kate."

"And sometimes you'd see her."

"Once we had lunch together. Once or twice."

Again I felt the hollowness, the ache.

"And you're certain you didn't run into her just before she died? I just want to know her state of mind."

Marc said, "She was fine when she left for her sister's?"

"Not really. She wasn't quite herself. There was something strange about her."

"And you let her go anyway?"

"I was her husband, not her lord and master. She was at her sister's in New York for nearly two weeks. You never saw her then?"

Now Marc's tone changed. "Why shouldn't I tell you if I saw her? Why should I try to hide this? Look, come to New York, spend a week, try to enjoy yourself. It's your last chance before I leave for Paris. I'll be there about two weeks before I return. I can introduce you to people here. I can introduce you to women if you like. Right now I'm not working, I'm bored to death because I can't find anything to write about," and I laughed. "No plots. No stories. No one going into a hotel." And I laughed again.

He gave me his address. I wrote down the number and the street. He said, "You can't miss it, really. It's just on the corner of Fifth Avenue. There's a green and white awning in front. There's a name on it," he said. "It's called the Vienna."

DIAL M

I had been there for some time. The bartender quietly said, "If you're going to sit here any longer you'll have to order a drink."

It was half past four. I recalled Denise's words exactly: *four o'clock*. Now I had no way of getting in touch with her. I felt ridiculous there, directionless, as though I were the victim of a joke. A middle-aged blond woman at the other end of the bar leafed through a newspaper, smoking cigarettes, endless cigarettes. Occasionally she'd lift her eyes to me with casual indifference, as though she had grown used to rejection and had retired from the world of temptation and pleasure.

Two men were at a nearby table, quietly talking business, trading gossip, the inside word on cotton futures. I got down from my stool and walked to the door. I looked up and down the street. It had begun to rain on my way into the city and now it was falling heavily, a dark slaty rain undisturbed by wind. The light of day was giving way to a deepening gloom. Not a taxi in sight. Not a car. No one.

I returned to the bar and ordered a martini and sipped it slowly. I said, "Do you have a phone here?"

The bartender indicated the sign for the public phones.

"I mean one where you can receive calls."

"Any call for me or my customers is routed through the hotel switchboard. Of course if you're a guest you can make all the calls you want through the courtesy phones and have the charges put on your bill. You're expecting something?"

I considered it. "No."

I pulled at my lip. I thought of Denise Casterman and the man who had struck her. I wondered if he was the cause of her delay. I looked again at my watch and shifted my weight on the stool and then she walked briskly in from the lobby.

She seemed out of breath. She shook out her hair and smiled at me in a familiar way, as though accustomed to seeing me often. She smiled and apologized and ordered a drink and then we moved to a table away from the bar.

She said, "Do you have your car with you?"

I nodded.

"Where did you leave it?"

"In the hotel's parking garage."

"Can you reach the garage without going outside?"

"Of course you can."

She smiled and lifted her glass. "Good."

I said, "Is something wrong?"

She smiled again. "David Reid," she said, as if testing the weight of the syllables. "You keep staring at me, David Reid."

"It's just," and I paused and lit her cigarette. "The last time I saw you it was at night. Now I have to get acquainted with you all over again." I gently touched the side of her face. "The swelling's gone down."

"The makeup covers it well enough."

"That man."

"My husband."

"You live together?"

"Not if I can help it."

"You can do something about him, you know. You don't have to put up with this."

"No," she said after a moment's reflection. "I don't have to put up with him. But right now I haven't any choice. I don't live with him and I'd prefer not to get you involved in this. I sometimes think," and she dropped it.

It was odd how much she resembled Kate: not in any precise way, not in detail, but rather in outline. The blond hair cut straight across. The soft angles of her face. The cool unreadable look of her eyes. I looked at her slim fingers, each nail perfectly shaped. She shifted her feet beneath the table and touched my leg with hers and kept it there.

"Yes, go on."

"One day my husband is going to kill me. He has a nasty temper, but that's not what frightens me the most. He's got a vivid imagination, he's created a whole other life for me. And he doesn't like that life he's dreamed up. He doesn't like it because he's not part of it."

"And is it true, what he thinks?"

"I don't know what he thinks. I just know he thinks it. He asks me for names, he asks me what I was doing two nights earlier, last Wednesday, a year ago when I was in Hong Kong. It's an obsession with him, he's out of his mind."

"And do you actually have a separate life?"

She said, "Of course I have a separate life, I have my work. I travel. I have friends." She looked at me. "Do you mean to say you're a writer twenty-four hours a day?"

I said, "But why would your husband want to kill you?"

"Because he's jealous of me. It happens all the time, doesn't it? They call it a crime of passion and the husband goes home free and washes the blood off his hands."

"Have you spoken to the police?"

"It's no good, I can't do that," she said. "He knows all the police. And I can't prove he's going to kill me. And he doesn't always hit me. Usually he's polite enough, he takes me out for the occasional meal, we go to concerts, he likes to be seen with me, it makes his friends envious. I go with him to keep the peace. And I'm not here all that often, the bank sends me from one city to another. I live out of hotels, it's part of my work. When I'm in Boston I almost always stay here. Last week I was in Philadelphia. And you know what? He followed me there, he kept his eye on me." She smiled. She seemed about to change the subject. "That's why this has happened, you see. Because I travel so much my husband suspects I'm having affairs."

"But you're not."

"Not at all."

"But the idea has crossed your mind."

"Once or twice."

"And nothing happened."

She shook her head.

"And you regret it," I said.

"Sometimes."

She was watching me steadily, her eyes on mine, betraying nothing. The fingers of her right hand tapped lightly against the side of her drink. Her left hand supported her chin. As if about to remove a speck of dirt I reached forward and traced the line of her jaw and she pursed her lips slightly. She was like an object made of crystal, hard and reflective, deceptively transparent; fragile. I wondered what it would be like going to bed with another woman, with Denise. In the two years of my marriage I had remained faithful to Kate, I'd barely even looked at anyone else. Now I felt as if I were on the brink of something, as if about to leave it all behind me, abandon it to memory: the house, the art college; my writing, my past: I was walking away from them. This single physical act, this moment of intimacy on a wet Friday afternoon, this alone would mark the end of one life and the beginning of another. Kate would be part of history. My history. Our history.

She said, "I asked if your car was here because I'd like you to drive me to the airport. I have to be in New York this evening on business."

"On a Friday night?"

"Banks don't stop business just for weekends, you know."

I thought of Marc's invitation, I said, "I'm also thinking of going to New York."

"Tonight?"

I hadn't thought about it. All I knew was that I wanted to confront Marc, learn the truth. There would be no recriminations, no debate. It was a simple matter of enlightenment. And once I possessed that, once I could understand why my wife stepped to her death, my life would begin anew.

"Tomorrow," I said. "Saturday."

"I'll be there. I'll be there until Monday morning."

"I want to see you."

A phone rang and the bartender picked it up and held the receiver to his ear. He turned abruptly and looked at us and spoke quietly into the mouthpiece.

Denise wrote down the name of her hotel. I said, "I want to see you."

"Yes."

"You know it."

"Yes."

She smiled and grasped her handbag and stood. "Let's go," she said, and the bartender hung up the phone as I walked into the darkness.

A NET, A WEB

Naturally you can't see her eyes.

She sits bent over her worktable, making lace. She works intently, her concentration is so tightly focused that she is aware of nothing but what her fingers are creating. She dominates the tiny canvas, she is the world. There are no windows or doors to be seen; the light comes from somewhere else. We are aware only of this young woman holding her bobbins, contriving intricacies. Yet it's not difficult to imagine her simple life away from the worktable: waking at dawn, preparing breakfast for herself, her sisters and brothers; sweeping the floors, opening the windows as the air warms. Possibly she has a suitor, an intelligent young man also from Delft, whose nose is always in a book; that is, when he is not looking at her.

She's a quiet young lady. She attends church, the Oude Kerk, of course, where in 1675 the artist who had created her would be laid to rest in his forty-third year. She goes for walks. She sees things when she looks out of windows. She glimpses intrigues among her neighbors, she trespasses onto the outskirts of them: the evidence of a raised voice, a hungry look, a shifting eye. She overhears lines of dialogue: she watches as a man steps from a doorway and follows another towards the curved edge of the canal.

Somewhere a voice says *Go. Go now.*

She keeps it to herself.

She sees a woman in the next house standing by a window reading a letter. In this house next to hers the woman begins to weep.

Does her detachment, as though she were an artist sitting aloof from the world, make her guilty of something?

Indifference?

Complicity?

Perhaps we've been misreading her. Perhaps her soul is tarnished, possibly she even enjoys watching the entanglements of others, the blossoming of individual dramas, the origins of tragedy in a letter received, a knock at the door, a withering glance. One day she sees joy on a young woman's face; and the next, a hollow look of terror.

What else has she seen?

Once she saw a man sitting at his window, painting the house where the lacemaker sits hard at work. Delft is thick with houses. One day the houses will crumble and be rebuilt, rails will be laid, a train will take people there.

The lacemaker makes connections.

Maybe I'm wrong. Perhaps beyond the act of lacemaking there is no life; nothing but the lace that will eventually emerge from a few bundles of thread: this is what her life is about, this indeed is her life, and that's all we know of her, all we behold. Like a spider she spins a web, and in that web is invested her life, with its hopes and fears, its small battles, the things she sees and the words heard in the night, whispered from below.

She has watched people rushing from houses and people standing by windows. She has seen those who cross courtyards on warm August afternoons, who smile and deceive; and those who smile and are deceived. In the intimate patterns that emerge from her fingers she has knotted them all, the artist and the wife, the wife and the lover, the lies and sad truths of her own quiet life.

THRILLER 1

It was late afternoon.

It had been raining that last time he was in the city with Kate. He remembered it because they had celebrated their first wedding anniversary there. A room was reserved at one of the better hotels. They booked seats at the ballet and ate at expensive restaurants. They went to an Alfred Brendel recital at Lincoln Center and saw a revival of the film *The Lacemaker,* starring Isabelle Huppert and set partly in the Normandy resort of Cabourg: Balbec in Proust's novel *A la Recherche du temps perdu.*

A young couple sits in an empty hotel dining room and looks through the windows at a deserted beach, the pitiless grey waves of the English Channel. Later, after he has dropped her, she will lose her mind and in a sanatorium spend her hours making lace and dreaming of other pasts, other futures.

For almost the entire week it rained, and like clockwork, at the setting of the sun each day, the rain stopped, only to resume at dawn. In all the years he had lived there the city had always seemed either bright and dry or hot and oppressive. Now it resembled London or Paris: a fixed grim scene of wet pavements and stained buildings and a lowering sky; a place where shadows merged and strangers stepped out of darkened doorways; where people disappeared, others went mad.

They walked to museums huddled under an umbrella, his arm about her waist. Their clothes smelled of damp, their shoes were sodden. Every evening before dinner they would undress and shower and have a drink and quite often make love, and in his memory he saw Kate lying beneath him, her head hanging over the side of the bed, her legs separated, her hand cupping her breast: unashamed, utterly erotic. And the memory nearly moved him to tears.

The street where Marc Rougemont lived was filled with shops selling paintings and old books. One specialized in antique optical instruments: telescopes made of bronze, astrolabes displayed in fine wood boxes lined with soft velvet. In the rear of the window, mounted on an easel, stood a reproduction of a painting of a man sitting at a desk. An open book was before him; the light coming through his window was no more than a pale yellow glow. His left hand gripped the edge of his desk, while two fingers of his right hand seemed intent on locating an image on a celestial globe. His delicate yet certain touch indicated imminent discovery, as if he were about to overturn a natural law or reveal how a distant star affected men's lives.

A green and white awning: the Vienna.

And instinctively he felt in his pocket for the postcard Kate had in her possession the morning she died.

The doorman told him that Mr. Rougemont had left an hour earlier.

"I've forgotten which apartment is his," David said, and the doorman took a few steps towards the curb and pointed to a window with his gloved hand.

"Do you know when he's expected back?"

The man shrugged.

He considered it. It seemed pointless to wait there for Marc. He looked at his watch. He thought of taking a taxi to a museum, the Frick for instance, where a day or two before her death Kate had stood and gazed back at a girl interrupted at her music.

At the deli at the end of the street he ordered a pastrami on rye and a bottle of beer and watched the only other diners there, two elderly women in hats and furs who ate their soup in silence and then haggled over the bill, their voices rising in anger, the waiter gazing upon them with bored contemptuous eyes.

When he returned the doorman shook his head.

It was the weather that seemed to have tired him. Because it reminded him of another, better, time, he felt slightly out of focus, as if his perceptions were not quite in synchronization, as if he were in a state of uncertainty; as if, and it occurred to him precisely this way, Kate's death had been an illusion; as though she had merely disappeared, her fate shrouded in doubt. As though he were living in one of his own novels.

He walked up the street. Denise's hotel was five blocks away. It stood there like a temptation, solid and welcoming and warm, windows upon windows holding mysteries, promising pleasure. The rain had become intermittent drizzle, driven by a stiff breeze. There was a chill in the air. He stood at the corner. People walked in and out of shops and restaurants. Men in tattered overcoats tried to catch his eye with their mad stares and mumbled misery. Police sirens howled and screamed three blocks away. He wondered if he would run into his ex-wife lugging her cello in its hard grey case, trying in vain to get a taxi. He felt sullied by this city, its endless rain.

When he returned to Marc's building thirty minutes later the doorman wasn't there. He'd gone off for a pee, a sandwich, or a smoke. David slipped through the door as other tenants were leaving. He rode the elevator and knocked on Marc's door and there was no response. He knocked again and then pressed his ear to it, and there was no sound except for the faint ticking of a clock. He listened to the scrape of his shoes as he walked over the softly lit checkerboard of the lobby. Now it was growing dark.

He felt foolish having traveled all this way simply to have a discussion with Marc. He wondered what impulse had driven him this far. It could have been done much more efficiently on the phone. It had been idiotic of him to hire a cab for the expensive ride from the airport. Things were building up, the stakes were obviously high. The accumulation of time seemed to urge him on. Someone lit a cigarette and walked out of a darkened doorway before disappearing around the corner.

He thought of Denise. When he rang her hotel he was told her phone was busy. He imagined the conversation, the gruff voice of her husband, *Who are you with, what are you doing.* Or else she had taken it off the hook, sending a signal to him: be patient. He pictured her in the shower, soaping her breasts, letting the water cascade over her. Her eyes were shut: was she thinking of him, were they at that moment linked in mutual speculation? He remembered the sequence of events that had led to his meeting Denise Casterman: seeing her in the restaurant beyond Marc Rougemont's shoulder; later when she sat in front of him in the cinema: little knots of coincidence. Odd how a shared glance had led to this. He crossed the road and stepped into the entrance of a small tourist hotel that faced Marc's building. It was a kind of insurance, taking a room there. The woman at the desk gazed at him as if trying to read his intentions. On the wall behind her a yellowing placard read, *Welcome to the Apple—Take a Bite of the Big One.* On the desk were stacks of leaflets advertising package tours, Circle Line cruises, the Statue of Liberty. It was obvious few of the rooms were occupied. She didn't even request that he register. She asked for the full amount in advance and handed him a key.

In the office an angry voice on a radio phone-in show said, *You need more than plastic surgery, lady.* The hotel smelled simultaneously of strong disinfectant and perspiration.

A man and a woman stood on the second-floor landing. She took a roll of bills from the man's hand and, stuffing it in her handbag, looked beguilingly at David and began descending, the man following her so slowly that by the time the front door swung shut he was still on the stairs, lighting a cigarette, humming contentedly to himself.

David's room was on the third floor. It seemed airless, as though it had been unoccupied for some time. He shut the door and looked around. The walls had absorbed unidentifiable stains; or else the light was creating alarming shadows, suggesting splashes.

Over the bed was a framed reproduction of a painting by Vermeer of a man standing at a table, a pair of dividers in his right hand. On the table was an unrolled map or chart. On the floor were two other maps, loosely furled. The man was gazing intently out his window, his head slightly lowered, as if he were taking the measure of something. David adjusted the painting until it hung straight, and his fingers took away dust.

Two small tables stood on either side of the bed, each supporting a lamp. In one of the drawers was a Gideon Bible, inside the cover of which someone had penciled in the words *The End: Came to Soon.* At random he opened it and read, *And then said Boaz unto his servant that was set over the reapers, Whose damsel is this?* In the drawer of the other table was a Manhattan telephone directory. Curiosity drove him to look up his former wife. There was no listing for a Michelle Reid, and he found that she had reverted to using her own name: Michelle Alpers. She was now living on West Eleventh Street. He thought of calling her, actually went so far as to lift the receiver, then hung up, ending all possibility of conflict and complication. The fewer people who knew he was in town the better. As though he sensed how the evening would end, how necessary it would be to remain obscure. The radiator went *hss* and again there was silence. He pressed his hand to the bed and then sat on it and immediately got up. He opened the closet and took an extra pillow out for himself. He switched on the television in the corner, watched the screen begin to glow, heard a voice say *Blanche of Navarre is dead,* then turned it off at once.

The bathroom seemed clean. He took a quick shower, changed his clothes and left the hotel, the woman behind the desk watching him with curiosity. The doorman said that Marc still had not returned. He took a pad of paper and a pen from his coat pocket, he said, "Maybe you'd like to leave a message?" and David said he'd prefer to see Mr. Rougemont personally. "I want to surprise him, you see. We're old friends," he added, and the words seemed full of sinister intent.

The doorman had a florid, open face. His smile was broad and toothy and somehow not quite innocent, the small network of veins by his nose hinting at drink. He pointed out that snow was predicted for that evening. "Two to four inches," he said, stretching his hands apart.

He walked through the streets and stopped at a grocery a few blocks away and bought a bottle of mineral water and an apple from an Egyptian man. He had the odd feeling of being displaced: not so much the sensation a traveler has of being in a strange locale, but that of having somehow shifted slightly off his axis, as if whatever changes had taken place had done so internally, affecting his view of things. Yet he also felt somehow depthless, perfectly calm, as though a decision had been reached in his mind that could not be altered.

When he reached Denise's hotel she was just returning from a meeting. She touched his arm and looked him in the eye and smiled. She said, "Let's have a drink."

The bar was quiet; only four or five tables were occupied, mostly by couples, or people concluding the business of the day, signing papers, packing their briefcases, toasting the conclusion of a deal with martinis or Manhattans. Denise had little to say. Her smile seemed forced, her eyes shifting distractedly here and there. When her look met his her smile softened, and once, beneath the table, she reached for his hand and squeezed it.

They went up to her room. She wore a pleated blue skirt and a white linen blouse; a strand of pearls. A faint echo of the perfume L'Heure Bleue hovered about her. For a moment they stood in the center of the room, by the foot of her bed, their hands before them, not quite touching, suspending the moment. Music was playing, probably on a car radio, a saxophone wailing against the restless doubletime of bass and drums, and then it faded as the lights changed and the traffic streamed down the narrow avenue. He took her face between the palms of his hands and brought his mouth to hers. A burglar alarm rattled unnoticed in the distance. He felt her tongue as it darted and jabbed against his.

She pulled away, she said: "My husband's followed me. Again." She could barely catch her breath.

"Is he staying here?"

"I don't think so. He wouldn't be so stupid. But I'm sure I saw him earlier outside the hotel. That was this afternoon. I haven't seen him since." She shrugged. "Maybe he's gone back to Boston."

"How did he know you were coming to the city?"

"I have no reason to lie to him."

"You're taking a hell of a chance."

She said nothing.

"I want to make love to you."

She said, "I know."

"I want to touch you, I want to hold you."

"Yes."

"Now."

"No."

"I must." He reached out and as though to convince himself

of her reality gently placed his hand on her breast, and through her blouse felt the heat of her.

"I have a dinner meeting. Then I'll be free."

"When?"

"Ten o'clock."

"I'll stay here with you. I'll spend the night."

She shook her head. "Not if my husband's in town you won't." She drew her finger along his cheek. "Come back at ten. Then we'll see," and she put her arms around his neck and pulled his body to hers.

‡   ‡   ‡

Now it was evening. The shops gave off a comforting light and he stopped often to look in the windows, at the books and shoes and furnishings, and sometimes he would glimpse his own ghostly reflection staring back at him.

He had forgotten to leave a light on in his hotel room and when he returned it took him a few minutes to find the switch. He turned on the television and watched the news. A tornado had struck a school in Tennessee: twenty-three children were killed; the principal said it was God's will and sent the survivors home early for the day. The severed head of an Oriental man had been found in a garbage can in the Bronx. A well-known sculptor in SoHo was arrested for making 4,735 obscene phone calls to Liza Minnelli. Still Marc had not returned, and when David went to the window to draw the curtains he realized that although he was directly opposite Marc's building he was two floors beneath the Frenchman's apartment; and to verify it he recalled how many floors the elevator had ascended, how many right turns he had made once he'd got out of it; precisely where the doorman had pointed when he'd asked. Other rooms were illuminated. A woman in a black leotard moved her arms slowly and laboriously and yet gracefully about her as though immersed in a tank of water. A man stood before a music stand, playing a saxophone. Another man sat at a desk facing his window, typing.

A man in a heavy overcoat stood talking to the doorman as he smoked a cigarette. He raised his left hand in the air and brought it swiftly down against his palm, and the two men began laughing.

David went down to the desk. Because no one was there he assumed the woman was in the office, listening to the radio or watching television. A voice said, *Exquisitely affordable . . . luxuriously yours . . . forever pink.*

David cleared his throat and banged his key once against the desk, as though he had accidentally dropped it, as if in reality he found it pleasant to be standing there, as if he had all the time in the world to himself. The woman stepped out and looked at him. She smelled of potato chips and cigarette smoke, and he could see he had interrupted her dinner. He said, "I wonder if I could change rooms."

Her eyes shifted momentarily to his chest and waist and then back to his face. "Is there something wrong?"

"Not really. It's just that I'd like to be higher up. Two floors higher."

Suspicion took the form of a furrow in the center of her brow. Perhaps she imagined he was planning to open a window and step out onto the ledge, eventually to hurl himself to the street below. She pictured detectives holding conversation with him before his death, negotiating for his life, trying to buy time. Priests and rabbis would be summoned, the fire department with their trucks and swiveling red lights and nets and ladders. Camera crews would be sent from the television stations, anchormen would speak his name at eleven o'clock.

"You want a room on the fifth floor?" she asked.

"But the same room. Do you understand what I mean? The same room, but two floors up. Look, I'm not going to," and she said she understood, there was nothing suspicious about it, she was just asking. She said: "It's not my business what the guests do. I'm trained to turn a blind eye." She exchanged keys with him and made a notation on a piece of paper. She said, "First time in the city?"

"I've lived here most of my life."

She paused. "You mean you live in New York?"

"I live in New England now. Massachusetts."

"Boston. Where the beans are."

"Near there."

"I have a sister in Hyannis, where the Kennedys live," and she looked at him with interest. "Are you here on business?"

He said he was there to meet an old friend. "Have a nice day," she said, and when David looked at his watch he saw it was nearly twenty to eight in the evening. At ten he would be with Denise Casterman. He thought of her body against his as they stood in her room. The taste of her mouth. The pressure and heat of her breast.

He wondered if Marc was intending to return that night. He imagined the Frenchman standing at the door of his house in Massachusetts at that very moment, knocking and calling for him, spying through the windows. He thought of the blue Mercedes and the phone calls that had ceased since he'd lunched with Marc. Things were beginning to make sense.

He moved his things to his new room and went to the window. Now he was directly opposite Marc's apartment: he counted the number of floors, looked down at the entrance to the Vienna, looked up. Yes: exactly across. In a room two floors above Marc's he could just make out the image of a woman changing her clothes, perhaps preparing to go out for the evening. In the yellow dimness of a table lamp she unhooked her brassière and stretched her arms above her head and looked out the window as she began brushing

her hair. There was something melancholy and unerotic about the
scene, as if it were a painting on a gallery wall, antique, thickly
varnished, a captured memory whose significance had somehow
been forgotten. Her heavy, wide breasts swung forward before she
pulled the shade and David lowered his eyes.

He shut the curtains and turned on one of the lamps. His new
room appeared to have precisely the same dimensions as his first.
In fact the furnishings were exactly the same: the two bedside
tables, two dusty lamps. A Bible, a phone book. It was the paintings
on the walls, reproductions like the others, that were different. A
woman in a bathing suit sits in a cramped hotel room, looking
disappointedly at a piece of paper, perhaps a timetable, possibly
not. Maybe it's a letter. She stares so intently at it that it's almost
as if she is trying to will the words to change their meaning.
Sunlight pours into the room, picking out the prim disorder of
unpacked bags, a toppled shoe, a robe over the arm of a chair.
And yet her face has turned darkly private in this narrow room,
where nothing remains but a window and a locked door, and hope
has no chance for a breath of air.

Night has fallen.

A man and a woman are in a restaurant in a city, sitting at the
counter, their hands nearly touching. Across from them, his back
to us, is a solitary man, possibly unrelated to them. The man who
works there, the man in the white jacket and hat, is preparing
something, perhaps getting a clean cup and saucer. Tensions can
be sensed, for while some have knowledge, the inside word, a hot
tip, a name and a number on a scrap of paper or book of matches,
others remain ignorant in this hellish world of smiles and betrayals:
the lines are drawn, something will happen, something dramatic
and unexpected, something sudden and terrible. The man will take
the woman's arm, he will lead her out into the street; and the
man who works behind the counter, the man in white, will watch

as the third man adjusts the brim of his hat and follows them into the deserted avenues, the shadows. And you will not even hear a whispered word, or the breath of a scream.

David opened one of the drawers in the dresser. It had been lined with shiny blue paper and smelt vaguely of cedar. In it someone had left a program from an off-Broadway play called *The Ice House*. The picture on the front showed a woman sitting in a chair, her knees together, reading a letter. David stood for a moment, staring at it before placing it back in the drawer. He walked into the bathroom and washed his hands and, returning, sat on the bed and opened the curtains so that a gap of only two inches existed. He watched Marc's window with one eye. He switched off the lights and turned on the television. A woman said, *I want him dead, Harry,* and immediately he changed the channel.

It was getting late; he regretted not having stopped for dinner. He felt oddly nauseated, imagining the grease from the pastrami smeared on the walls of his stomach, the coiled miles of intestines. Images on the television flashed before him: people sitting at consoles with numbers displayed before them, like code breakers trying to identify fragments of words exhibited on a screen; a man and woman walking hand in hand through a field; a little boy eating a breakfast cereal, talking to his mother; a man in a car, loading his revolver with gloved hands. He continued switching channels. Over scenes of mounds of corpses, a tower of skulls, a voice recited, *Whereof one cannot speak, thereof one must be silent.*

Now something caught his eye and he leaned forward, gripping the curtains with his hands, holding them taut as a light was suddenly switched on in Marc's apartment and then a woman entered and immediately he thought: *Denise.*

She crossed the room and unbuttoned her coat. Through the thin translucent curtains the detail was remarkable.

Denise. But it wasn't Denise, it was impossible. David had just seen her, touched her, held her, and the more he watched the more he realized that it was only someone who looked like Denise, who therefore appeared to be Kate.

Marc and Kate; Marc and Denise. A story lay somewhere between the two phrases.

Marc had always liked that type, it somehow satisfied his tastes: blond, severe; cool. How predictable people were: their lives could be reduced to patterns and diagrams on a page, each revealing an appalling symmetry. The dazzling complexity of a piece of lace.

His breath condensed on the window. Marc entered the room, smoking a cigarette. David began to reach for the phone and then withdrew his hand as he saw the woman pick up Marc's phone. Marc stood beside her, saying something. He sipped from a glass and handed another to the woman and then he looked directly across at David, but only apparently so, for he could have made out nothing but the darkened façade of an empty hotel.

There were footsteps on the stairs outside David's room, voices, a man and a woman speaking in fragments: "I'm tired." "Yes." "I've been on my feet all day." "Yes I see." He listened to them enter the room directly above his. Though refusing to believe the woman with Marc was Denise, he felt somehow more enraged by her presence, for it brought Denise to mind: therefore Kate. He could follow with precision the strange logic of it, as if he were rapidly ascending a stairway, two and sometimes three steps at a time.

In another room the man continued typing at his desk. Cigarette smoke gathered above his head in the narrow beam of his lamp, curling upon itself like liquid before dissipating. Marc touched the woman's cheek and kissed her on the mouth, and when he lifted his hand to touch her face David found himself inexplicably lifting his hand in the air, mimicking the movement.

Denise would be waiting for him at ten.

Kate was dead, mingled with the air.

The world is independent of my will, said the voice on the television.

Now they disappeared from view, and although he could no longer see them he could easily imagine what was happening. He shut the curtains and went back into the bathroom and squinted against the pain of the light as it came on. He felt as though he were suspended above the law, beyond the limits of responsible behavior. Watching, waiting, speculating; preparing. He thought of Kate, whose death was unnatural, whose death was like a rent in his life, an anomaly; or like something imperfectly seen, as out of the corner of one's eye, something that would forever perplex him.

He wondered how long the woman would be staying with Marc. He felt his palms moisten and he rubbed them against the towel. He wondered if it was worth waiting to hear the truth. It was not the waiting that was in question, but the truth. Did he truly need to know it? Was it akin to finishing a long novel in which one has been fully engrossed? In time would it really matter? Was there something within him that demanded to see the fine print of Kate's last days?

He pictured her standing at her desk, the letter between her hands: he could recreate in his mind the light in the room, the expression on her face, the look of her hands.

He remembered her sitting by the window in the restaurant, looking out towards the lake, lost in the rippling sunlight on the surface of the water. A terrifying stillness, a stillness that begged to be disturbed, as though it were a sheet of paper waiting to be torn.

He returned to his seat on the edge of the bed and parted the curtains. The woman in the leotard pressed her hands together above her head and slowly began to separate them, defining an arc. The saxophonist fingered his instrument, hunched his shoulders. There was no movement in Marc's living room. The man at the desk continued to type. The apartment belonging to the woman who had been undressing was now darkened. A light was on in another flat, and he could see a woman sitting in a chair, watching television, slowly eating a meal from a tray. She picked up a telephone receiver. She nodded her head, she turned aside, she spread her fingers in a gesture of anguish. She hung up and then took a napkin from her lap and held it to her eyes, each in turn.

A word, a look, a phone call ripen into the small dramas of others' lives; like an explosion spreading outwards towards the past and the future.

David grew alert as the blond woman came into view and Marc helped her on with her coat, holding the two sides of it in his hands, pulling the woman towards him, touching her lips with his, playing with distance. She tossed her head back, making her thick blond hair move: a familiar gesture, one he had seen before, years earlier in London. She began moving away from Marc, saying something to him. Then he saw the woman come out of the building and onto the pavement; and for a dark moment David saw Kate leaving Marc the morning she killed herself.

And then she walked away, just as Denise had that first night in Boston.

INTERMISSION

Within seconds you grow uncomfortable. You're strolling in the Frick and suddenly you come upon this painting and the woman has turned to look at you as if to say, *What is it?*

You've disturbed her, you see: the scrape of your shoes across the floor; or perhaps it was when you cleared your throat, jingled some coins in your pocket. Or perhaps you had meant to be quieter, you'd planned on the element of surprise. First you checked the bedroom: nothing. Then the dining room: no one. The kitchen was also deserted, save for a girl who had drunk too much wine and was having a nap at the table, lost in her dreams.

Where is she?

Where *is* she?

And who, may I ask, are *you?*

A servant? A neighbor? Perhaps you're her husband. You've come home early from work on this lovely Delft afternoon and lo and behold what do you see but your wife in a room with another man. She sits in her red jacket; he stands, towering over her. He's showing her something on a sheet of paper; her instrument, possibly a lute, lies on the table. It looks like a music lesson, and you've interrupted her. The man's left hand, which is not holding a piece of paper, rests in an intimate fashion on the back of her chair. Music, is it?

A lesson in harmony.

Her lips are slightly parted: perhaps it's the prologue to an exclamation—*Oh!*—or merely a soft unspoken *Ahh,* the dying embers of a smile.

Yet it all may be perfectly innocent. She'd always said she wanted to take up an instrument, study music. For those long winter evenings. For when you were away.

But there's more here than meets the eye. Look again, look at the painting hanging on the back wall: a cupid holding a playing card. It was a familiar emblem in Vermeer's day; he used it once again, in a painting of a woman standing at a virginal. Its motto is *Perfectus Amor est nisi ad unum.* Perfect love is for one lover.

One lover: you, or *him?*

Just a moment. We've run across this man before. He's the one trying to force a glass of wine on a poor half-drunk woman in another painting. He gets around, doesn't he? Perhaps he's friends with the man who wears the red jacket, the man who invades the homes of married women while their husbands are off at work, buying paints, out for a stroll, or simply traveling abroad for a week.

You can almost see him, knocking on doors in the early afternoon, you can just about hear him: *Perhaps you would be interested in a music lesson, madame?*

Almost certainly he has a reputation as a good musician and a respected professor, he's had great success in encouraging the inartistic to tap their natural abilities to pluck a string, depress a key. He begins with simple tunes requiring little dexterity, standing beside his students, indicating the rhythm with dainty movements of his hand, sometimes singing quietly along, *ta-dee dalaa,* stopping them with a word, an upraised finger, when they've lost their way. Occasionally, holding his face close to theirs, he points out an interesting turn in the music, how a shift occurs in this measure or that; the labyrinthine nature of the fugue.

He's a big man, isn't he. Heavyset. And though his eyes are lowered to the sheet of paper he's sharing with the woman we can read much into his expression. This is a man who knows precisely what he's doing, who's aware of what he wants, who is quite capable of handling himself in any situation. He'd as soon throw you down the stairs as look at you.

Under his breath he might be saying: *Remain calm. Let me handle this.*

But that's not what's troubling you, is it. It's *her* expression. She lifted her face to you just as you entered the room, she turned and presented you with a face you'd not seen before; she's looking at you and yet you're not quite there. Where are you?

More to the point, where is she?

THRILLER 2

Once again it came to him: a subway platform; the roar, the impact, and then darkness. Over and over he imagined it. The smell of metal, the appalling whine of the brakes. Her life had been wasted in less time than it took him to conceive it.

He picked up the phone and the woman at the desk said "Yes?" and then he hung up and realized it was better this way. He put on his jacket and left the hotel.

The doorman was not there to impede his way, offering chitchat and meteorological observations. He buzzed one of the other tenants, no one responded, tried another, then when he was free to enter went up to Marc's door and knocked lightly on it. Things grew vivid for him. He could hear music coming from another apartment, a Bach partita played on the violin. In the distant background a saxophonist practiced scales. A spoon rattled in a teacup. Someone laughed. He knocked lightly on the door. Marc said, "Just a minute, please," and when he opened the door a moment later he looked at David with a smile frozen in surprise. He said, "I didn't know."

"You don't mind?"

"Of course not, I."

"I'm not interrupting anything?"

"No, I'm just packing. I'm flying to Paris in the morning." He pulled the door open wide, he began to laugh. He said, "I'm glad you came tonight and not tomorrow, you would have missed me. I'll be gone for two weeks, actually."

"Paris," said David, without quite knowing why.

"I'm also going to do some traveling. I've been invited by friends to their place in Rome. I may go to Amsterdam for a few days."

He wore a red cashmere sweater and jeans. David noticed that grey had begun to appear in his hair.

"Are you sure I'm not disturbing you?"

"No, no, come in."

Marc took David's leather jacket and tossed it over the back of a chair as if it were a rag. Through the bedroom door he could see an open suitcase, clothes piled beside it. Though small, the apartment was expensively decorated. Books in both French and English stood precariously stacked on the floor. Magazines and newspapers lay here and there. Framed prints hung on the wall alongside paintings Marc had bought in his first lush days of success. A nude woman lay across her bed. A slash of black intersected a patch of white.

There was a taste of cologne in the air, a scent familiar to him, the smell of Kate, of Denise, an ambiguous twilit odor. "You weren't alone, then?"

"Did I say I had been?"

"A woman?" And they both began to laugh.

"A good friend. A journalist from Paris. She just flew in yesterday. You know, you really should have called first, I," and David said, "I didn't know I'd be here until this morning."

Marc took out two glasses and made them each a drink. He looked at him: "Have you eaten?"

"More or less."

"I've already had a meal, but if you want to go out I'll sit with you if you like. If you wish." His accent seemed stronger. David wondered if this happened every time Marc prepared to return to Paris, if he discarded all the American traits he had so happily acquired over the past year. Or did they give him a certain cachet on the café terraces of Montparnasse?

"Thanks anyway."

"Are you sure? There's an excellent Thai restaurant just around the corner."

"I had lunch at the deli at the end of the street."

"God help you, David Reid," and he placed his hand on his shoulder and they both laughed.

When asked where he was spending the night David remembered the name of the hotel where Kate and he had stayed on their anniversary, far from Marc's apartment.

Marc went into the kitchen and opened the refrigerator. He said, "You could have slept here, you know. I'll let you have the key, if you like. I'm leaving first thing in the morning. I'm afraid I haven't much to eat. Some olives. A few grapes. Hearts of palm."

David felt as if he were detached from the reality of the moment, aware of himself, aware of the drama about to unfold, though not quite within it, not yet a participant. He could not imagine how things would develop, what words might come out, the nature of Marc Rougemont's reactions. And yet the air was rich with inevitability, with the relentlessness of time, a strange undefinable necessity seeming to hang over them, as though Marc had foreseen his arrival, had known what was on his mind, guessed how the evening might unravel.

David said, "I'm flying back to Boston tomorrow. I only came here to see someone. A friend."

"A woman?"

He laughed and thought of Denise. "A woman."

"Good for you. I'm glad. It's probably just what you need, something to distract you, to get your mind off things. Something new. You know. You know what I mean."

For a few moments they looked warily at each other. Marc broke the silence, he said, "What is it, what's wrong?"

"Kate was here for two weeks before she died. I'd like to know if you saw her during that time."

Marc lifted his hands in a dramatic gesture of bafflement. "So you think I had something to do with Kate's death?"

"In an indirect way."

Marc rose from his chair, he said, "That's absurd," and he tipped some more Dewar's into his glass. He lit a cigarette. David imagined Marc and Kate together, and then he thought of the funeral, and Marc's strange silence. He thought of a blue Mercedes snaking behind him along the twisting deserted roads. The midnight phone calls, and those that came just before dawn.

"You sometimes ran into Kate here in the city. It's a funny thing," he said, as if thinking aloud, "but there's something not quite right about all of this."

" 'All of this'? All of what?"

"Kate's death. The fact that sometimes you used to see her."

"I used to run into her occasionally. That was all. What, do you think I was sleeping with your wife?"

"I just want the truth."

David began to walk around the room, looking at the books, the records, the framed prints on the walls. On one shelf stood copies of Marc's novels in their various formats and translations. Over the desk was a large photograph, stunning in its detail. It had been taken on a beach, there was wind in the blond woman's hair; behind her was the façade of a large hotel, undoubtedly someplace in France, possibly on the Normandy coast.

Not a cloud in the sky. One imagines her eyes picking out a distant boat, a speck on the sea, following it until moved beyond the curve of the earth. David lifted a hand without quite touching the photograph.

It all seemed to bring to mind Kate; not the Kate he knew but rather a potential Kate, the one that might have been: fulfilled in her life, a mother, the successful translator of novels about people who enter hotels, who stand by windows and witness things.

Marc began speaking of his trip to Paris and then David said, "Were you sleeping with my wife?"

Marc looked at him.

"I asked if you were having an affair with Kate. It doesn't matter now, there's no need to hide it."

"Kate wasn't well, you know," Marc said. "She wasn't quite," and he sought the word with his fingertips.

"She was pregnant, you mean," he said. He felt perfectly calm, master of himself. "If she was, you did it."

"Look."

"Shut up."

"Look. I'd always been attracted to Kate, of course," Marc went on. "I'm sure many men were, she was a very beautiful woman, your wife. But she was," and again he tried to find the word, "she was, I don't know, unhappy. *Mélancolique.* You did nothing to help her."

David went to the window and looked down at the street. He looked across at his hotel.

Mélancolique.

Mé-lan-col-ique.

In the room beside his a curtain shifted and the light was switched off. He said, "How often did you see her?" and Marc turned to him.

"I don't remember."

"Did you sleep with her?"

Marc said nothing.

"But you saw her. You saw her here."

Marc touched his forehead with his fingertips, as if he were suddenly in pain. "Yes."

"Before she died."

"Yes."

"More than once?"

"Once or twice, yes. More than that."

"And in Boston."

"Yes. Yes. She was so unhappy, you know."

"You took advantage of her."

Marc walked to the desk and as though he were alone began sifting through some papers. He said something to himself, a whisper, something in French. The distance between them was mutual: David watched him as though scrutinizing a painting in a museum, trying to grasp the subtleties of its structure, the relationship of one detail to another, the iconography of the work. He listened to Marc's words, to the spaces between them, the nuances and second meanings, searching for euphemisms and slips of the tongue.

The room seemed smaller as he came nearer to Marc. Quietly he said, "What did she tell you before she died?"

Marc looked at him. He said, "Do you mean did she say she was intending to kill herself? No, nothing like that."

"And you never made love to her."

There was a long pause. Marc shrugged.

"Yes or no?"

"I don't know what to say to you, David."

"Tell me the truth."

"Look. I couldn't bring myself to do it. She was so vulnerable, you see."

"But you would have."

"Of course. She was a very beautiful woman, a very intelligent woman. But I never took it that far."

"Because of Kate or because of me? Were you afraid of betraying a man you barely knew?"

Marc smiled and lit a third cigarette. "But she was in love with me." And he said it with such an air of nonchalance that it was like a line from a song, a smoky afterthought escaping from the lips of an Aznavour.

David returned to his chair and drained his glass. He poured himself another drink as if he were settling in for a long relaxing evening, as if he had all the time in the world. He could feel anger like waves of nausea rising and falling within his chest. Marc had been allowed a privileged glimpse of Kate in the days before her death. It seemed unjust, pathetic, that David should have been so excluded from her agony.

He thought of Marc in the city, in this apartment; always with Kate.

A man walks into a hotel, he parts the curtains, he sees things.

"Didn't it occur to you that she might be on the brink of suicide?"

Marc swung around suddenly and stared at him. "You think I caused it, don't you."

"The idea never crossed my mind. It's just that you spoke to her before it happened. I simply want to know what she was like, what her mood was."

"Just what you said. She was depressed."

"Did she say anything about her health?"

"I don't remember."

"You had meals with her?"

"Yes. A few."

"You took her here. You took her to your bedroom."

"Once, yes."

"You took her to bed."

"I told you, I never."

And David said: "You began to make love to her."

After a pause Marc said, "Yes, only that. She seemed perfectly willing."

"You touched her."

Marc said nothing. He seemed pleased with himself.

"You kissed her."

Marc said nothing.

"You touched the buttons of her blouse."

"Yes. For God's sake, yes."

"You couldn't keep your hands off her, could you."

"She didn't mind."

"What are you saying, that she wanted it?"

"She told me she was tired of things. She told me she needed a change. That's why she came here. That's why she came to me. She loved me, David."

"She said this?"

"That was why she was here."

He imagined the two of them together: in restaurants, in city parks, in a bedroom. The next time he saw her she was smoke rising from a brick chimney. He felt as if he had never really known her, as if for much of their marriage they had been stepping slowly away from each other. "You brought her here. You kissed her, you began to undress her."

Marc suddenly turned to him, he said: "Look, David," and he wet his lips with his tongue and began to seize the air with his hands, as if taking hold of a globe, "she undressed herself. She came to me."

"You made love to her."

"Yes."

"You said you hadn't."

"Yes."

"But you said."

"I wanted to spare you the details. The truth."

"You made love to her. But you never loved her. You fucked her, you mean."

"She wanted to do it with me. She told me you were suffocating her, you were making it impossible for her to," and he looked for the word, he plucked it out of the air, he said, "you wouldn't let her live. She was like a work of art, you couldn't see her as a person. She was an image, an icon to you. She felt like something you'd created, you wouldn't take your eyes off her, you wouldn't let her breathe."

He stared at Marc through his tears. "She told you this."

"Yes. Many times." He seemed about to add something else, when he said, "Look, I have an early flight tomorrow, I must pack."

"Tell me more."

"I've told you enough."

"You phoned me late at night to hear my voice. You followed me and nearly drove me off the road. You probably got some sort of kick out of this, then."

"What?" He seemed genuinely surprised.

"You rang my number and said nothing. You tried to drive me off the road with that Mercedes you rented."

"You're insane."

"You killed my wife. You drove her to it."

"You could have done something to help her, David."

"You followed me."

"No."

"You rang me up, you called me. You wrote her a letter asking her to come and see you. A letter in a blue envelope."

"It's your fault she died, not mine. She couldn't decide, she couldn't make up her mind, you were making things too difficult for her."

There was nothing he could say. Kate had told Marc things that she should have reserved for him, her husband. All the certainties of his marriage fled him in the hour he spent there. Kate had fallen in love with Marc. David had become the Other Man.

His anger became mixed with a profound sadness, a sense of opportunities lost, of violation. Marc lifted his hands in the air. He said, "I'm sorry, David. I am, you know."

David looked at him. "She never got beyond the first page of your book."

"There was too much involved, I suppose."

"You're a bastard."

And he said nothing.

"How long?"

"What?"

"How long had it been going on?"

"A while."

"Did you know her back in London?"

"No, no, nothing like that. It began when I first came to see you at your house. But," and David looked at him. "It was very strange but we realized we had met once in Paris, quite a few years ago. She lived there, you know."

David said nothing at first. "She never told me this."

Marc gave him a startled look. "That she lived in Paris?"

"That you met there."

"We have a mutual friend. There was a party in Montmartre, on the rue Choron. It was very odd, what a coincidence."

"But it started when you came to see us in Massachusetts."

"More or less."

David stared at him. "You mean you did it in my house. In our bed."

"It just began then. This attraction. That's all. She phoned me a few times after that. We became friends."

"Then you fucked her."

"Look."

"And what else did she tell you? That she wanted you to marry her?"

Marc appeared startled, he raised his hands in the air, he said, "Yes, she said that, we talked about it that last time."

Suddenly it became difficult to breathe. "You mean she was thinking of leaving me."

And Marc nodded.

"And what did you tell her?"

"I told her I couldn't commit myself to her. That I had other friends, other women. But we had talked about this before, you see."

David stared at him. "So you toyed with her. You kept her on a string. Then she walked out and threw herself in front of a subway train."

"Stop this, David. Stop it."

He took Marc's arm and squeezed it and Marc pulled away. David felt something within himself letting go. Time became something heavy that rolled uncontrollably down a steep hill. He remembered the phone call from Josie telling of Kate's death, the blinding light that filled his head at that moment. He thought of the terrible emptiness that lay within him. He came to hate Marc as he stood looking at him, his laughing eyes and careless ways. He felt as if he were trapped in a small room and people were standing outside, mocking him, his grief, the darkness of his life. He began to pull at Marc, to shake him, to wrestle with him, not with any purpose in mind, but more as if he simply had to grapple with something no longer abstract. Marc slipped away and he followed him out of the room. Neither of them ran: it was as though they were simply going through the motions of pursuit and flight, as if it were a moment that required no genuine commitment; and yet something vast, something somber and oppressive, seemed to be filling the spaces of the apartment, overwhelming them, guiding their hands.

He stood and watched Marc as he seemed to be looking for something, tidying up, plucking at things on the kitchen counter. Marc said something in French, then told him to get out, and as he came to lead him to the door he began to fall backwards and slip on his heels. He grabbed onto an open drawer as if to support himself, the drawer slid out and fell to the ground with a crash and as his hand came away it held within its grasp a knife and it began hacking at the air, as if to strike at David, to stab him.

Now David felt himself separating, as though mind and body had no part in the debate of one or the other. He watched himself as he held Marc down on the kitchen floor, I watched him smiling at the superiority of his position. He pressed his hands against Marc's throat and saw the smirk disappear as the look of fear and hollowness rose to his face. Marc's hand sprang open the same moment his eyes shut. David grabbed the knife and stood and then in no more than a whisper Marc again said, "Get out." His face was red and seemed swollen. With difficulty he got to his feet.

David said, "I must know more." Again he imagined Marc making love to Kate. He saw him sitting on the edge of the bed, smoking a cigarette, extracting confidences from her, wondering aloud why she had married a man like David. He saw the sunlight on the floor, the wall, he could hear the noise of the city behind her moans of pleasure, the Gallic urgings of her lover.

The Details.

"Tell me," he said.

"She wanted it. It had nothing to do with me." He began to move towards the bedroom, as if to resume his packing, as if nothing at all had happened, was about to happen. He followed him, grasping the air, trying to get hold of the man.

The bed. Now he was in the bedroom, looking at it.

He looked on it with horror, as though it were a scene of carnage, a site where people had been sacrificed, where people had suffered, and the thought of it made him feel tired, more than tired, for the fatigue that had been gathering for most of the long day now lay like an immense weight upon him, as time must to a dying man. By killing herself Kate had heaped on him all her confusion, her grief, the ache. He felt somehow diminished, astonishingly ordinary, standing in Marc's apartment, as though he had been stripped of his clothes, his possessions, his identity; reduced to pale nudity.

"You're lying," he said. "Everything you say is a lie. Before this you said that you only ran into her once or twice here in the city. Now you tell me you actually took her to your room. Where is the truth?"

"Get out."

The knife was still in his hand. They began to move into the living room, Marc walking slowly towards David, his hands raised as though to protect himself. "It wasn't supposed to happen this way," he said, his voice full of fear, and David could see himself holding the blade, he could see what was about to happen. He came closer to Marc, he felt himself stepping beyond a limit, as if through a door into a darker, more lucid region, he slashed the air, back and forth, seeming to come nearer to the answer. "Liar," said David as he moved forward.

Marc dropped to his knees and looked up at David imploringly, as if nothing that was happening made any sense, as if he were a child faced with an ineluctable mystery: an eclipse of the moon, a war.

There was blood on the floor and walls. There was blood on David, on his shoes and hands, and the room filled with a bitter metallic smell. It was like a dream, as if he were in some odd way watching himself staring at Marc, seeing him and yet not seeing him at all, as if a sudden white light had entered the room. Nothing complex was taking place at that moment. It was a simple, primitive emotion he felt, and he remained frozen a few moments more.

The curtains in the living room were still open. David switched off the light and went to draw them and for a moment looked across at his room, the narrow flickering glow from the television he'd left on. In the window above his a blond woman and a man stood talking. The man lifted his hands and tried to touch the woman, to hold her, to draw her to him. The woman shook her head and turned away. The man slowly stretched out his hand and began to pull the woman towards him, and when she turned away again he seemed to strike her on the side of the face, because she flinched and touched her fingers to her cheek. Someone in the room next to his lit a cigarette in the darkness, the tip of it an orange glow as he sucked at it. Bits of conversation came back to him, *I've been on my feet all day. I'm tired. Yes I see.* It didn't matter who said what to whom, only the memory of the voices, words echoing in a deserted corridor, lingered in his memory. The couple turned and seemed to look at him. He could hear someone typing in another apartment, and the image of a man sitting at his desk and smoking came to mind.

He was still no better informed of his wife's last days. Perhaps her last days had begun a year earlier, when she'd first met Marc. He had told David conflicting things. Maybe he'd never slept with Kate; all the time he'd ever spent with her was in professional conversation, discussion about the translation, about people who see things from windows. Possibly Marc had lied because in truth he was a cowardly, lonely man who hadn't much luck with women. Kate wasn't alive to dispute his testimony. Perhaps he was a fantasist, a shell of a man who lived on dreams and hypotheses, who kept his distance from the world, who only imagined, in all its roundness, in all the warmth a writer is able to muster, the passionate life that might have been.

He shut the curtains. He looked down at Marc. He felt both liberation and ruin. But all that came to mind was a painting of a woman weighing gold in the dying light of day, the scales in exquisite balance.

THE REFLECTION

We've been here before. She seems awfully familiar. In fact she was in Kate's flat in London, putting on her strand of pearls. The smoky haze of afternoon fills the window. She's standing by the table and looking at her reflection in the mirror on the wall, and we're moved to pity because her face glows with happiness and anticipation: she is in love.

She is in love and we know that over this love hangs a cloud of disappointment. Yet we must allow her to savor this moment, we mustn't deny her this: it's what she's been waiting for all her life. When she's with him things are so very different, she feels something within her letting go. She has read her books of poetry and only now can she comprehend what words like *passion* and *love* and *bliss* truly mean. But see how pretty she looks! In her hair is an orange ribbon, tied neatly into a bow. She wears her pearl earrings and a yellow jacket trimmed with fur, and she's about to finish putting on her pearl necklace.

Look well, because we will not see her again, not in this life.

Where is she going?

Meet me. Meet me by the elm tree.

On the table is a brush of some sort.

Meet me. I must see you.

Beside it is a card or piece of paper.

Today. This afternoon.

Now.

And she thinks.

And she thinks.

Look again at the card or piece of paper. It lies on the table, flat save for one edge of it, the edge that's facing us. As if it's about to whisper.

Look at me! it hisses. *Look!*

Her affair with this man hasn't been all smooth sailing. They've had their ups and downs, their little tiffs, their disagreements. He's written to her before, and the news hasn't always been good. This time things are different.

I must see you.

Today.

Now.

She wants to look her best. She feels everything depends on her appearance, her mood, her reactions. She examines her face in the mirror and at the very instant she secures her pearls to her throat the sunlight pours in through the window, spilling like fresh milk onto the wall behind her. It's a perfect moment: the happy conjunction of thought and image, nature and artifice. And when her eyes meet those in the mirror she sees that she is beautiful, she achieves self-recognition, she has become what she wants others to see of her. In her own way, she's become an artist; because an artist is always reflected in her work, dressed for the occasion, showing off her best side.

The mirror has seen service elsewhere. It has hung before the woman who weighs pearls and gold, who indeed does it in this very room; except then it held no reflection, since the woman with the balance was not lifting her eyes to look at herself. Interesting: the pans of her scale were empty and the mirror left unfilled.

And perhaps even the artist himself had used this same mirror when painting his portrait sitting at the procuress's table, this portrait of a man who has somehow missed the point.

Or has he?

That expression of his . . . Perhaps we're misreading it. *Is* he missing the point? Or is it, rather, that he's harboring a secret. Perhaps what he's trying to tell us is that he knows precisely what is taking place in his household, virtually under his very nose, and that what is taking place has a bad odor about it. He knows, and nobody knows that he knows. He will watch and wait for further developments.

Or else.

Or else he's simply picturing it all, inventing things. Possibly she has inadvertently dropped a hint, or he's come across something on his wife's dressing table. An envelope. A clay pipe. A trouser button dropping into the pond of his imagination; causing ripples.

We've seen reflections before: when she was reading that letter, for instance, and her face was broken into four panes of glass, four segments of a troubled expression; though we're denied the opportunity on this occasion. Only the woman putting on her pearl necklace is allowed to glimpse herself in the mirror, only she is permitted to consider herself.

But this is a woman who when night comes, will not return to this room where the sun washes the wall with light, where the mirror holds her smiling face.

It's late afternoon, as it always seems to be. Autumn, and the leaves have turned yellow in this rust-colored city. She approaches the big elm near the canal, and in his eyes she's a small figure growing rapidly larger. She can hardly keep herself from breaking into a run, and he smiles to himself because he has always been irresistible. He sees her jacket, the fur trim; the sunlight as it picks out her pearl necklace. He steps out from behind the tree and her heart leaps with joy. He smiles and touches her cheek with his fingertips.

Calm down. Relax. Rest a moment.

From her window the lacemaker watches them, remains impassive, returns to work.

From his window the artist sees the man in the red jacket, he sees the woman talking to him, he sees the lacemaker through her window, he turns away and meets his image in the wood-framed mirror.

Now they begin to walk along the canal. Time begins to move quickly; soon night will fall. The moon will rise and the man in the red jacket will go out with his friends for a drink. Maybe he'll gamble a little, perhaps even make a killing at the card table. Possibly afterwards he'll pay a visit to the brothel. He feels lucky. He feels lucky because he has no conscience, no memory. One day he will think back to this day and he will try to remember the woman's name; and it will have eluded him.

In the morning two boys on their way to school will notice something yellow in the Vrouwenregt canal. They will come closer and begin to scream, for what they have seen troubling the reflection of trees and sky is the body of a woman. A woman who has died of disappointment, whose alternatives have run out.

Yet something of her will survive, if not in the mind of the man in the red jacket who stands behind the procuress, coin in hand, waiting. For all of eternity she will be utterly caught up in her reflection, in this brief second of happiness while she ties on her pearl necklace, while she parts her lips in a smile that grabs us by the heart forever and ever.

CAMERA OBSCURA

Where is the truth? Is it somewhere between the eye and its reflection, in some unseen middle distance, midway between the flat polished surface of the mirror and the glossy convexity of the lens? Or perhaps at the point at which image and word meet as one?

Does it lie in some obvious place, as a purloined letter sits unconcealed on a desk and so remains paradoxically obscure to us?

Possibly the truth is a sound, a deafening roar or something whispered. A word that strikes like the flat of a sword against the side of the face. A word that gives us vision, puts things into perspective, stuns us into sight.

Can it be found rather in some no-man's-land between an exchange of words, in the long silences that also have their place in human discourse? Or would I suddenly stumble upon it in the cracks between the pictures and details I was unable to suppress from my mind?

Maybe it's all located in the writing, in the curves and serifs streaming out from the pen; the dots over the *i*'s, the crosses of the *t*'s. Or pinpointed somewhere between the reality of a scribbled sentence on a sheet of blue paper and what our imagination, for lack of evidence, has made of it.

Meet me. I must see you.

Today. This afternoon.

Now.

Or is the truth in the balance itself, at the point in which both trays of the scale are equal?

It was nearly ten. The few people out huddled together for warmth, trying to keep their balance. The air was filled with a dense snow that seemed to muffle the sounds of the city, to scatter light from the lampposts. Even in the hush and beauty of the moment the city was decaying. Dust and newspaper tumbled down deserted streets. Bodies lay crumpled and unconscious in doorways, sometimes voices cried in the distance. Lovers, their arms entwined, became lost in each other's desires. People whose mad eyes stared at me in the lamplight. The sky lowered, trapping the stink of day. Buildings of grandeur became shadows, haunted malign gaps in the world.

On the corner of the next street a crowd was gathering. The police had already roped off the area. They engaged in pithy conversation with their two-way radios and moved about in a fidgety uncertain manner, gesturing broadly, raising their voices. A woman had fallen, and a few members of the crowd pointed to the window, a distant dark rectangle, the blue edge of a curtain blowing in the breeze.

She lay sprawled on the sidewalk, so vulnerable, a blonde like Kate, a pretty woman. The strand of pearls she'd been wearing had fallen from her, become twisted into something like a question

mark just to the right of her head. Her hands lay palms upward
by her side, her fingers slightly curled, as if they belonged instead
to a small child. The expression on her face seemed placid; there
was even the trace of a smile. A vague sense of warmth seemed
to rise from her body, as if, instead of having suddenly deserted
her, life was taking its languid time, departing in stages, coyly,
reluctantly; carrying with it final images, final thoughts, last
moments.

Snow continued to fall, a sad dry snow on a cold night, the
end of autumn. Other people walking by stopped and stared and
clicked their tongues and made little noises as they tried not to
look at the obscenity on the ground, the mingling of beauty and
death, the face of mortality: the terrible mystery of expiration.
This wasn't a scene from a thriller, not the orchestrated death you
see in a film, the awful crescendo of murder, the words and images
surrounding it; and the hushed reality of it was horrifying. Perhaps
for these few minutes we were sensing the value of our lives, the
prickling of our skin, the blood coursing through our bodies; as
though the weight of the day had been lifted by this woman's act.

She couldn't have been much older than Kate was when she
died. There was little doubt she had killed herself. Standing on
the sidewalk her neighbors spoke of her unhappiness, the aura of
hopelessness about her, her solitude, their words obscuring the
reality of the tragedy, enclosing it like a blanket. She'd been a
musician, a pianist, forever on the brink of recognition. Yet in her
expression there was no hint of despair. Despair was an expression
of the living; that night it was reflected in the frightened eyes of
the bystanders, in the litter on the ground, the way people shuffled
their feet, the words they used, the look of the buildings amidst
the rubbish and the rumors and the snow.

Soon someone would miss this woman; someone who had been
waiting to see her, or hear from her; someone who had no reason
to doubt she was still alive. Or possibly there was no one; and the

thought found an echo in my memory. I gazed up at the open window and walked away.

Winter, far too early, had arrived.

Denise's hotel was a tall modern building, its hundreds of windows bright against the dark sky; identical to other hotels in other cities, beneath other skies, each room duplicating the next with its blue carpeting and Bible and drinking glasses wrapped in paper. I wondered if she would still be there. I imagined her husband catching up with her here in the city, where cries went unnoticed, where people disappeared without a trace. I saw the man lifting his hand, striking her in the face, staring down at her as in a daze she clumsily tried to get back on her feet. I thought of the woman on the sidewalk and wondered what in life had driven her to death, what tiny moment that night had pushed her to the ledge, what word or thought, what news.

Yet Denise was alive, and that night she would be with me, she would love me.

Or would she? Perhaps she had returned to Boston. There was the chance she was with someone else, someone she had come to meet, someone she had met, and as I considered it I realized how little I knew her, how elusive and ungraspable she was, how dependent on her I was growing. To Denise I was just another man; for me she was the beginning of countless possibilities.

I rang her from the courtesy phone in a booth just off the lobby. I watched the man behind the desk pick up the phone. When I asked to be connected to her room his head swiveled around until his eyes met mine. She said she would be down in a minute, and I hung up and sat in a chair in the lobby and the man continued to look at me.

I watched the elevator doors opening and closing. People returned from restaurants, from shows, from rendezvous, glutted, slightly tipsy; others were on their way out, moving in a rush to the doors, their eyes fixed on the dark street outside as they fled towards midnight. Here there was no stillness, no ambiguity. I thought about the woman I had seen in Marc's apartment, how she had brought to mind Denise and Kate. It seemed strange that only now was I feeling the real pain of her betrayal; now that Kate was no longer here to answer my questions, confirm the details.

Now I wanted her more than ever before, I wanted to start over, go back to the pub in Bloomsbury two years earlier, as though we were in a novel demanding to be rewritten.

I felt as though I had come to the end of a life that had begun in London that Wednesday afternoon; and when I thought of that day, of our lunch in the pub across from the British Museum, it was as if I were trying to recall a chapter in a book read long ago, and of which I had retained only the barest recollections. The richness of her laughter, the way she looked me in the eye: these things remained vivid. I could still just make out her face across the table from me, I could see her smile, I could sense the chill in her, the otherness of her, the mystery of this woman I eventually married and lost; the screen of words that stood between us.

I hadn't noticed Denise until she was standing by my side. She pressed her hand lightly against my shoulder, lifted it to my neck, touched my hair, let go. How long had she been there, watching me watching for her, waiting, remembering?

Quietly she said: "You came."

And when I stood and reached to touch her face she stepped abruptly back. "I'll buy you a drink," she said.

A man at a piano in the bar played a medley of old songs, "I've Grown Accustomed to Her Face" and "The Night Has a Thousand Eyes," a tall lean man grinning to himself as if within his mind he were repeating some private joke, some observation, or else mocking his audience as they flirted and drank and lost focus.

We sat at a table. She pressed her lips together and looked at me. "Another wasted trip." For a few moments she said nothing more. I ordered our drinks.

She said, "I deal with my bank's trust customers. Most of them are extremely wealthy, very important people, people you read about, you hear about. When they want something done they want it done when they wish, where they wish. That's why I'm always traveling. Some refuse to deal by phone. They're not business people. They're," and she paused, "they're just rich people. They establish foundations, some of them even set up charities. Most don't know very much about money, investments. Most don't even know what's in their portfolio."

She seemed barely aware of me. She lit a cigarette. For the first time in three years I took one for myself and savored the smoke as it filled my lungs.

She looked carefully around the room, scanning the faces, watching for people in the shadows, beyond the glass doors. The bar was crowded, the music barely audible over the rising volume of conversation. I could see the head of the pianist gently bobbing over his keyboard. A woman stood by him and whispered something in his ear and he lifted his face and laughed. One of the bartenders held a cocktail shaker above his head and agitated it.

She said, "A lot of it's old money. Boston money, Beacon Hill money. These aren't people with fax machines and computers, they want to read all the fine print and ask me questions about their transactions and then sign only when they've decided we're not trying to cheat them out of their millions."

I imagined her having spent the evening with Marc Rougemont. Perhaps they had made love before dinner, undoubtedly she couldn't keep her hands off him, possibly they had even begun on their way up to his apartment, in the elevator or the stairway. I pictured her on her knees, undoing his trousers. *I love it when you do that. I love you.* And I found myself desiring her all the more.

I thought: *There is nothing I wouldn't do to have her.*

She shrugged, she said, "It's just that this time, with this customer, I couldn't convince him that our investment strategy would be beneficial."

"So what happens—you go back, you get your hand slapped by the bank president?"

"No. It's just."

I looked at her.

"It's nothing," she said. She seemed disgusted.

She seemed unwilling to look at me, to acknowledge my presence. I felt my desire for her shimmer and agitate like the surface of water, as though about to evaporate. Oh yes, I still wanted her. But I wanted the Denise who earlier had pressed herself to me, drew a finger across my cheek, let me touch her breast.

I said, "A woman killed herself just a few blocks away. She'd thrown herself from a window. I saw her."

She stared at me.

"I saw her on the ground. It must have been ten minutes after it had happened. She reminded me of my wife. I couldn't take my eyes off her. Whether it was because she was dead or so much like Kate, I don't know."

Denise chastely touched my hand and I looked at her. "I suppose I might as well go back to my hotel," I said. It was a lie.

Now she looked at me. "No, stay."

"But you don't even seem to know I'm here."

She touched my hand again, she grasped my fingers. "Yes I do. I do, really."

"I want you."

"I know."

She reached down and opened her briefcase and took out a copy of my latest novel.

"You mean you actually bought it? Nobody buys my books."

"But of course I did."

I was stunned. "It must be love."

"I just finished it this afternoon. I liked it very much. I really did."

"Say that again."

She laughed. "I liked it a lot."

"A great deal?"

"Yes."

"Look at me. Turn your head slightly to the right. Tell me: you couldn't put it down?"

"No."

"Really?"

"Really," she said, laughing again as Kate materialized across the table from me. This time I wouldn't lose her.

I inscribed the book to her and she put it back in her briefcase. She said, "You look tired."

"I am." And she waited. I said, "I almost killed a man. The one my wife was seeing. I had to see him, I had to talk to him, to find out what had happened between them. I could easily have cut his throat."

"Are you serious?"

I smiled, I said, "I almost did. That's all."

"But you didn't."

"I wanted to."

"But you didn't."

I paused. "No."

"Tell me. Tell me the truth."

"I wanted to kill him. I could imagine myself doing it, I could see it." And the scene blossomed in my mind: blood on the floor, blood on me, on my trousers and shoes and hands, the room filling with a bitter metallic smell. I could see Marc's eyes, which would begin to lose their sheen, their reflective quality, as he lay lifeless on the living-room carpet.

I remembered moving towards him, the knife in my hand, and it was as though I were writing it, it was like a scene from one of my novels, one sentence following another, overpowering Marc, taking the breath from his lungs.

"For one moment, actually for longer than that, it was more like ten minutes, I saw nothing wrong in my killing him. It seemed almost right, the only proper thing to do. No, that's not it, it was," and I tried to find the words, "it was more a necessity, something that had to be done, that was required."

She said, "But you didn't do it."

She looked at me and shifted her leg until it rested against mine. I tried to picture what she looked like without clothes. The silkiness of her skin, her slim waist, the curve of her thigh, the weight of a breast. But I didn't just want her that way. I was entranced by her, I was as caught by her as I had first been captivated by Kate. The more she kept her distance from me the more I wanted this woman body and soul; and I seemed unable to learn my lesson, because I had said it before. And undoubtedly I would say it again. One last time.

"Maybe you know him?" I said. "A Frenchman," and I watched her expression carefully. "Marc Rougemont."

Nothing. Not a flicker of an eyelid. She shook her head.

She said, "Could you have done it, killed this man?"

"Possibly."

"Would you have felt any better?"

I thought about it. Somehow my grief for Kate seemed to abolish all sense of morality. It cast a shadow over the problems of the world, over my sympathy for others, it swept from my mind the certain consequences of my act. When I thought of Marc and Kate walking into his apartment, when I imagined her giving herself to him, when I heard her words echoing in my mind, nothing else mattered but to destroy the man who had ruined my marriage, who had stolen my love for her, who had pushed her beneath the wheels of the train.

The artist is a murderer.

She continued to look at me, at my eyes, as if seeking out the answer.

I said, "Probably I would have."

"But you didn't do it."

"No."

"And you're sorry."

"I don't know," I said. "I don't know."

"You can't spend the night with me," she said.

"I know that."

"I told you why."

"Yes."

"It's not safe."

"I know."

"He was there tonight, following me."

"He has no right."

"I wish he were dead," she said, looking away in disgust. Then she turned to me and very quietly added: "It would be an end to this, you know. He'd be out of the picture. Then I'd be free to spend the night with you. We'd have time. More than one night." She touched my hand and parted her lips slightly. "All I can give you now is an hour."

I didn't know what to say, I shook my head as I tried to get the words out, I said, "Yes, all right."

She finished her drink, put down some money, and was out of the bar before I could join her.

She was waiting for me in the lobby. As we rode up in the elevator she said nothing as she watched the numbers on the panel light up and then fade. She stood close to me and I could feel the heat of her body through her clothing. I wanted only to put my hands on her, to feel the texture of her, the solidity of this woman. For too long I had been living with a ghost.

But I could see there was something wrong, I could see it in her eyes as her attention shifted this way and that. When we were inside her room she shut the door and leaned against it. "What happened tonight with my client," and she looked away. She seemed to be weighing something, she said: "Everything had been arranged in advance. Even his attorney had urged him to conclude the deal. We were about to purchase some real estate on his behalf. He couldn't lose on it, he knew he couldn't. Give me a cigarette."

She looked through her bag.

She'd left them in the bar, she said, "Fuck."

"I'll get them."

"Forget it."

"Denise——"

"You know who spoiled this? My husband. I knew it would come to this, I knew he'd begin to get involved with my work. Christ."

"But."

"I could tell. I knew it the minute my client said it. He'd received information that the value of the property in question was going to fall. I asked him how he knew this. He said that an anonymous source had told him earlier today." She looked at me. "That's my husband for you."

"Does he know I'm here in New York?"

"I don't know. I don't think so."

"What if he did?"

"Then he'd probably put two and two together and kill us both."

She looked at my face and then she looked at my body. She said, "Switch off the light and open the curtains. It's too bright in here."

I pulled open the curtains and when I turned she put her hands on me. She slid my jacket off my shoulders and began to unbutton my shirt and then she took my hands and placed them on her chest and I unbuttoned her blouse and felt in my palms the lace of her bra, the heft of her breasts. I unhooked it and dropped it on the bed and in the neutral cold glare from the street lamps, the light falling upon her in geometric shapes, wedges and arrows and stripes refracted by the window, colliding and merging on the surface of her body, I could see her breasts, the curve of them, their shape, small and round and perfect. I held them gently with my hands as she began to unfasten my trousers. I undid her skirt and she stepped out of it and I could see her legs, long and slim and yet muscular. With one hand she touched my cheek and with the other she held me and felt me stiffen and I slid my hand inside her panties and then the phone rang.

Instinctively I stared out the window, to the darkened windows across the road, as she placed her hand over my mouth, as if to stop me from speaking. She picked up the phone by the bed and listened. And then she hung up and looked at me.

Night fell. Midnight arrived.

Time passed.

THE OPEN WINDOW

Can it be late afternoon?

The light is so uncertain, isn't it, in the painting called *The Little Street*. Possibly because of the clouds that are beginning to gather, low over the city of Delft.

Let's assume it's late afternoon.

We see a brick building, an adjoining passageway, other buildings near and far. We must be standing at a window, possibly the second-floor window, for we can look down and see a woman sewing in the entryway to a house, and to her right, another woman leaning over a barrel. Are those children kneeling on the ground, playing on the walkway in front of the house? Or are they really two women scrubbing the tiles, gossiping, whispering: *Did you see? Did you hear? Well I never . . .*

All the windows are shut; autumn is approaching, there's an ocher chill in the air.

A calm domestic scene.

All the windows but one.

Look.

Look at the upper-right corner. There's a window open, but we can detect nothing but darkness. If it was nighttime, and a candle was glowing in the room, we would undoubtedly see all manner of things, though from our perspective they would be mere shadows, dark uncertain shapes shifting along the walls, bleeding across the ceiling. Now, however, we can only enter a realm of conjecture: we can see nothing; or, if we like, we can see everything.

‡   ‡   ‡

It's late afternoon. The light coming through the window discovers a woman standing at a table weighing gold and pearls. The pans of her scales are empty. Behind her hangs a painting of the Last Judgment. What is she thinking? Is her mind on her work, on the precision of it, on those who rely on the accuracy of her balance, the quality of her eye?

Or does she wonder about the baby she will soon have?

Whose baby is it?

‡   ‡   ‡

A woman is at an open window reading a letter. The words in the letter fill her head with grief, time begins to press heavily on her shoulders and her mind seems to be going in four different directions.

‡   ‡   ‡

A woman sits at a table, waiting for a coin to fall into her open palm. The artist stares out at us. Who are the other men? Are they really there? Perhaps they're ghosts; or just memories, con-

jured up by the woman's mind. So who, really, is the artist in this
scene?

‡   ‡   ‡

A woman is tying on a strand of pearls, watching her reflection
in the mirror by the window. This, we like to think, is a woman
without worries, in complete possession of herself.

She's putting on her pearls because she's about to go out to
meet someone.

He waits for her by the big elm near the canal. He stands and
smiles to himself and watches the water, and when he knows she's
approaching he moves slowly out from behind the tree, a red blur
appearing as if from thin air: coup de théâtre!

Her heart leaps; she's been looking forward to this moment for
a long time, she feels beautiful and soon, she hopes, she will once
again feel loved.

There is no such thing as love. Things move inexorably toward
disappointment. Things wear off, run down, break, or decay.
Things die, or simply disappear; people walk away.

‡   ‡   ‡

A woman and a man are in the room. The man's red jacket is
draped over a chair. His hat hangs from a wooden hook.

Through his trousers he gently fondles his genitals.

Sit on my knee, he says. *Kiss me.* He grips her bare arm and pulls
her towards him. Now he will have her. He will have her clothes
off in an instant and he will have her as he has had every other
woman he has met: whenever he wants, however he likes it.

Or possibly he won't have her; not today. He will bring her to
the peak of anticipation and then walk away, go home, leaving her
frustrated and anxious for his next visit.

He lives in a world that is devoid of pain and pleasure. He is an inarticulate man, not much more than a pretty face who finds his relief in brothel and salon alike. Women pity him a little, they call him *poor boy,* they like to mother him. And because he is empty he can be whomever he wishes. Haltingly he can tell tales of his life, of his experiences in the wars, and women listen to him because he's attractive and has a low voice and always, always on the border of his recollections is embroidered *I have suffered.*

He presents himself as being uncomplicated. He goes hither and yon, wherever the whim takes him. He says he is hunting for happiness, true happiness.

Will you provide it for me? he wonders aloud, and who can resist such a line?

But he doesn't want happiness. He lives in a world of mirrors. He wishes to be recognized, he needs to see his reflection in the eyes of others, especially women, because if he doesn't he disappears. For he is nothing but a shell. And when the shell goes unreflected and unrecognized there is nothing.

Zero.

‡   ‡   ‡

The Art of Painting, wrote Samuel van Hoogstraten in 1678, three years after Jan Vermeer's death, *is a science for representing all the ideas or notions which the whole of visible nature is able to produce and for deceiving the eye with drawing and color.*

‡   ‡   ‡

A man and a woman are in the room. The woman lies on the bed as the haze of late afternoon falls on her body. The man watches her intently, for the combination of her nudity and the weak sunlight removes her from the sensual realm, transforms her into texture and curve and shadow. She is no longer a person, no longer a woman who weighs pearls and gold, who reads letters, who dozes and dreams in the middle of the afternoon.

The artist sees only shape and shadow and the qualities of the light. Later he will see her as his wife.

‡ ‡ ‡

A man and a woman are in the room. This is the man who had written to her. This is the last time he will see her, he explains. He wears a red jacket and has left his hat on his head, for he can stay only a moment. The woman sits on the bed, weeping into her hands.

He shrugs and moves the shiny toe of his boot in a small arc across the floorboard. *Hss,* it whispers.

Her husband knows nothing, she thinks. She's tried to avoid looking into her husband's face; as though images of her straddling her lover or lying beneath him, whispering endearments, her bare breasts quivering in the light of late afternoon, might be seen in the blue of her eyes, like so many pictures hanging in a gallery.

He seems to see everything else, doesn't he. He watches and he paints, and when she does look into his eyes all she can see is herself, twice over, in the brown depths of them. It brings to mind the murky uncertainty of the Delft canals, or deep wells into which others have fallen. Look carefully: see them looking up at you.

‡ ‡ ‡

The artist is sitting in his studio, gazing out the window, watching the woman leaning towards the barrel, the woman sewing. He's all alone. He thinks his wife has gone off to do some errands. His head still aches from his night out with the boys. Yet he's painting and watching also the open window, through which he can see only the interior of his mind, the brittle creatures of his imagination:

a woman weighing pearls and gold;

a woman tying on a strand of pearls;

a woman reading a letter;

a woman interrupted at her music;

a woman making lace; others.

He paints them in such a way that their thoughts are unavailable to us.

Always on the verge of action.

Forever about to utter a word.

What word, what action?

WINTER

Though the storm had dwindled to flurries by the time I left Denise's hotel, it must have continued snowing in Massachusetts for hours afterwards. Instead of a painless two inches there was nearly a foot of it by the time I arrived the next afternoon, drifted up against the front of my house, weighing down the branches of the trees. Fresh footprints, larger than mine, led to the door, veering off to the window before curving back on themselves to the road: a question mark left by the mailman, the woman who reads the electrical meter; someone seeking a view. When I reached the front door my feet were soaked, my legs were freezing. I listened to the texture of the silence, the familiar denseness of it.

Go.

Now.

And for a minute I remained motionless by the window as she looked at me.

Go now.

I could still see her, standing by the telephone in the darkened room, beyond the reach of the streetlights. A police car, its siren wailing, raced past the hotel. Someone walking outside her room said, *But it's a frame, darling,* and Denise began to dress.

The light in the house was a chalky combination of grey sky and the whiteness of snow, reminding me of the students at the art college preparing their canvases, scrubbing them into neutrality with gesso. The platform where the model usually stood was empty. A short, grey-bearded man with paint on his shirt walked from one student to another, making quiet suggestions, pointing, gesturing.

You're digging into things other than what you're seeing.

Over my desk a woman holds a balance, her eyes averted from the world, from damnation and salvation.

In the bedroom a woman ties on a strand of pearls, her only reality her image in the mirror.

The artist lifts his brush.

Where is the truth?

The book Kate had given me was on my desk. I opened it and the woman whose music lesson had been interrupted looked at me as though daring me to cross the line, break into her world, alter her expression. To disrupt the moment like a sudden wind.

The stillness of the house was like a balm to me. For the first time since Kate's death I felt the necessity for solitude, the pleasure of seclusion. I told myself it was best I hadn't grown too involved with Denise. With her husband following her, watching her, capable of tremendous violence, we would always be under his scrutiny, we would never be alone. The city, the world, were rapidly shrinking.

Go.

We quickly dressed. As though afraid of being overheard I said under my breath, "Come with me."

"No."

"You can't stay here."

"We'll leave separately. I can go to another hotel."

I thought of the room I had taken, opposite Marc's apartment. I tried to imagine what I would see when I looked into his window. Would he be pacing, drinking, drawing his hand through his hair; wondering when I would return to finish the job, exact my revenge? I could see him standing at his window, watching me watching him. Perhaps he would be with a woman, a blonde, touching her hair, drawing her to him. Or he had already forgotten about what had happened, returned to his packing, switched off his light and fallen asleep.

"Stay with me," I said. "Just for tonight." She slowly shook her head, aware only that she'd never be free. Her husband had followed her, he had seen us go up to her room. She came to me, touched my arm, pulled me to her before shutting the door quietly behind me. And when I returned to my hotel room and looked across at Marc's window I saw only a darkness that defied interpretation.

He'd be out of the picture. Then I'd be free.

If he were dead.

If he were dead.

In order to see the web the light has to be at just the right angle.

The stillness in the house: there was something unfamiliar about it, as if absence of noise could be classified by degree and retained in the memory. I shut the book. It was as though someone else were there with me, out of my sight, watching, waiting. I turned slowly and looked through the doorway into the bedroom. I could see the foot of the bed, Kate's desk with its computer, her books on their dusty shelves, the framed snapshot of a little girl standing apart from her parents: the definition of emptiness. How much of this was in her mind the moment before she let herself go, before she took that step off the platform? Had she in that instant re-created this world she was about to abandon, was it her last thought, a frozen tableau of an interior, our bedroom, the photograph taken at her sixth birthday party, Marc's book lying on her desk? My shadow as I stood watching her?

Or could she only hold on to the image of a letter on blue paper, taut between her hands?

The light from the window was so even that everything seemed on a single plane, as flat as paint on a canvas. I listened and heard nothing, and yet I felt a chill run through me, as if a breeze were moving steadily through the house.

But all the windows were shut.

‡   ‡   ‡

She phoned me early the next morning, her voice reduced to a whisper, strained with urgency. I was surprised to hear from her; or rather I knew that were she to call me I would succumb to her, once again involve myself in something delicate and unstable; something beyond me. I felt for Denise the kind of desire Kate had never elicited in me. For my wife I had felt love. Love was an underground spring, a vein of gold running deep in the earth, inherently permanent. For Denise I simply felt desire, as though it were something electrical, something potentially fatal that surged through the arteries of your body, lifted you from the ground.

She was a version of Kate, perhaps even the Kate Marc Rougemont had known: passionate, alive, hot to the touch. Yet all I remembered of my wife was a woman self-possessed, silent and distracted. If only she had shown me both sides of her; if only I had been able to see them. If only I had been someone other than me.

She said: "I must see you. Today."

I looked out the window. More snow was predicted, and you could see it in the way the clouds lay, heavy and low, vast smudges overhead.

"Now."

She was calling from a hotel in Cambridge. She'd never stayed there before. Just this once, she said, just to be safe. To be someplace where she wasn't known. She was certain she hadn't been followed. Things were getting dangerous.

"It won't take you long."

"Come up here," I said. "Rent a car. Take the train. Stay with me."

For a moment she was silent. She repeated the name of the hotel, and when she again asked me to drive down I could hear it in her voice: the panic, the helplessness. I looked at my watch.

Driving along the back roads that led to the highway I listened to a tape of the guitarist David Aurphet playing Bach's lute suites as I moved rapidly past the riding stables and schools and mansions. The farm stands, only a few weeks earlier dispensing pumpkins and Indian corn and jugs of cider, were shut for the season, only to reopen in early December selling Christmas trees and wreaths. This would be my first Christmas alone since Kate's death. There would be no tree with strings of lights and delicate glass ornaments, no late-night drink on Christmas Eve, no exchanging of presents in the morning, the floor strewn with remnants of green and red paper, silvery lengths of curled ribbon. I would wake up to just another day. I would sit at my desk and try to write, or I would sit at my desk and think about trying to write. I would sit at my desk and do nothing because Kate had left me bereft of words.

And then a few weeks later I would have to return to the college.

The snow began just as I got into Harvard Square and pulled into the parking garage beneath the hotel. I took the precaution of calling Denise from the courtesy phone in the lobby. She said she'd meet me in the concourse below, where there were shops and restaurants, an open eating area filled with people, potential witnesses.

When she stepped out of the elevator I could see what had happened, why she was so frightened. Under her dark glasses her left eye was swollen nearly shut and the side of her face was bruised. She wore jeans and a sweater: I'd never seen her so casually dressed. She seemed so much smaller, so much more vulnerable. She pressed herself to me. She began to cry, but soundlessly, her body trembling against mine, and a few people sitting at the white plastic tables looked up at us, prepared to misinterpret the scene.

We spoke in whispers.

"He beat me up."

"Shh."

"I thought he was going to kill me."

She grew calm. We bought coffee and sat at a table. "When I walked out of the hotel he was waiting for me. He," and she looked away. "He pulled me into a doorway in a side street. He punched me."

"No one saw you?"

"He kept hitting me."

"Where did you stay?"

"The same room I was in. It was pointless to go anywhere else." She took a compact from her bag and stared at herself in the little mirror. "God, I look awful. I haven't been able to go to work."

"You'll have to tell the police. You can get a restraining order. Then he won't be able to go near you."

She shook her head and took hold of my hand. "It won't make any difference." She laughed to herself. "He's a judge, David. And you know what cases he deals with? Divorce. Divorce," she said again, letting me savor the irony of it. "Now he knows about you. He saw us together."

My eyes grew wide. "Does he know my name?"

"I don't know. I don't think so. Maybe." There was a look of panic in her face. "Everything he's imagined has come true."

"Your infidelity."

"Yes."

"Another man."

"Oh yes."

She seemed about to add something. She pressed her lips together and shook her head, as though to rid it of a disturbing thought. "It's my fault. I saw you in the restaurant. That's all."

"And then you followed me."

"I'm sorry," she said. "This has nothing to do with you, this should never have happened. You've been through so much already." And she looked away. "Your wife dying like that. I barely know you. It doesn't matter. Just forget it, forget you ever met me."

I watched her leave the table. There was no hesitation in her step. She was walking out of my life, back into a world of suspicion and madness, where curtains parted in darkened rooms. I watched the elevator doors slide quietly open. I slipped in just as they began to close.

Though it was normally a forty-minute drive it took us nearly two hours to reach the house. Until we got on the highway she was uneasy, watching other cars as they passed us. I said, "Do you think he knew where you were staying?"

"It's impossible. But with my husband you never know."

I glanced at the rearview mirror. The driver of the black BMW behind me wore dark glasses and was smoking a cigarette. "What does he drive?"

"A Mercedes," she said. "A blue Mercedes 380."

The snow had begun to accumulate. Things were becoming precarious. A few cars had skidded off the road. Everywhere there were police cars, tow trucks. A helicopter passed overhead and disappeared from view. I did a steady forty: I was in no rush. I savored this ride, every few minutes turning to look at Denise, to convince myself she was there beside me. No one could touch us, not here, not now. She slept nearly the entire way, her head resting against her window. I listened to a tape of the Brahms cello sonatas Kate had bought me for Christmas a year earlier, and the velvet mournful sound of the instrument brought my wife slowly to life for me, a woman inwardly grieving, withholding tears, caught in a net of deception. How long would it be before I completely understood Kate, before I could see with clarity, put into words, the contradictions of her life? And would it only be then that I would be free of her?

That look of contempt; the way she excluded me from her world: a bleaker, darker world whose terrain I couldn't begin to describe. Words had become as fluid and uncertain as water.

"We're here," and I touched her face.

"No."

"Wake up."

"No," she cried, opening her eyes.

When she saw me she smiled, and her smile moved me in its sadness.

"We're home," I said.

She'd brought little with her to the hotel: a suitcase, her briefcase. I took them out of the trunk and she held my arm as we hiked through the thick snow. She stopped for a moment, the flakes falling about her. She said, "It's so quiet," and gripped my arm tightly as I unlocked the front door.

I watched as she looked around the narrow living room, at the prints on the walls, the few pieces of furniture Kate and I had bought at secondhand shops in Essex or borrowed from our landlord. Although I had lit the wood stove earlier, and the house was warm, she kept her coat on as she walked from one room to the next and then back to join me. On my desk was the photograph of Kate I'd taken at Martha's Vineyard. She picked it up: it was as though she were looking in a mirror.

"I never knew her," I said.

I watched as she went through the doorway into the bedroom.

She stood for a few moments at Kate's desk, looked down at Marc's book, rested her fingers on it, turned to me.

"What is it?"

And she said: "Nothing. It doesn't matter."

‡   ‡   ‡

By nightfall the snow had begun to fall more heavily. It was when Kate was happiest in the house, when nature was beginning to trap us and we were inside where it was warm and the lights glowed and music played. Now Denise and I were safe; no one would attempt to drive on a night like this; no one would come near us.

She was restless, she continued to walk around the house, touching things, leafing through books, the Vermeer album Kate had given me; the novel by Marc. She brought it into the living room and sat beside me on the sofa. The name *Rougemont,* thick and black against a white background, struck me in my heart like something solid, as though all my pain, my sorrow, were bound up in those nine letters. She said, "This is the man you told me about, isn't it. The one who'd been having an affair with your wife."

She turned to the first page, she extracted a line: *"Tombée de la nuit."* She looked at me. *"Minuit."*

"You speak French."

"A little. I had to learn it for my work. I told you, I sometimes have to travel to Europe, the Far East. I've studied German, Italian, enough Japanese to make an impression. Have you read this?"

"I can't read French."

"And your wife was translating it."

"She didn't get very far. I suppose things got in the way."

She looked at me. "Things."

"Meaning him."

"Meaning her affair."

"Meaning," I said, "her affair."

She set the book on the table, she said, "My husband . . ."

I looked at her.

"You saw how he was at the restaurant. At the movies. He just doesn't give up. When I'm at the bank he calls me four or five times a day, asking me what I'm doing, where I'm going, who I'm seeing. At work I suppose he's a different person. Impartial, dispassionate. He listens to husbands and wives accuse each other of incompatibility, of adultery. Cruelty." She shrugged. "He watches children cry as their families fall apart. He's got a wonderful reputation, of course, someone like that always does. I married him ten years ago, when he was a prosecuting attorney. He was a good lawyer, an attractive man, a nice man. He's very bright, his mind can hold so much, he can pull all the threads together in a complicated case. But he won't divorce me, because how would that look? Just think what it might do to his shining reputation."

"So you just carry on with it."

"Only as far as I have to."

"Do you sleep with him?"

"Sometimes. Even though we're separated he won't admit it to anyone. So I usually spend one or two weekends a month at the house. He takes me with him to dinner parties. He says it wouldn't look right if he went alone. In bed he's tender. A little vulnerable, even. In a funny way he's very much in love with me. But when I'm traveling he's like another person. Always questioning me, always wondering where I've been, what I've done. Where I'd slept the night before."

"So why don't you just leave him? Leave the state, go to a different city?"

"He'd find me."

"He can't be that powerful."

She smiled and rose from the sofa. "You don't know my husband."

She took my hand and led me into the bedroom. She switched off the bedside lamp. I could feel her hands on me, pulling my sweater over my head, undoing my jeans. Very quietly she said, "Please be gentle with me."

When we got into bed she lay against me. I held her face in my hands and kissed her lips and she began to cry, her tears on my cheek as I comforted her, my hand moving slowly along her bare back. Within minutes we were asleep, our bodies pressed together, her leg over mine. Nothing more happened; nothing more was needed.

It was just past midnight when the phone rang; two days before the letter arrived.

I saw you.

PORTRAIT OF THE ARTIST

Sometimes the artist sets his mind free in a labyrinth of speculation.

Everything contributes to it: his long hours in the house, sitting before his easel by the open window, in the silence of the waning day. His hearing is acute; sounds reach his ear. Such as church bells. Such as voices in the distance, those of children, the laughter of men who have drunk too much, who stagger and wheel by the edge of canals.

Listen: a passing cart, the hooves of horses, *clopclop clopclop*.

He also hears the shutting of doors, he discerns footsteps on the stairs outside his studio, steps that come to an abrupt stop.

A whisper: or is it only the wind, rising up over the coast from the North Sea?

His wife has assured him on more than one occasion that the house is haunted, and at times he has noticed things: doors left ajar when he was certain he had shut them; a lighted pipe by the fireplace, when it had been a day or two since he'd enjoyed such a pleasure. *Hss,* says the ghost.

Silly boy, she says. *Don't fret so.*

And she touches his hair and lifts his chin with her fingers, and he smiles in that funny way he has, with bafflement and mirth.

Usually the house is noisy, though, especially in the mornings, when the children invade the rooms, break into his studio, beg Papa to let them make a picture. They dip their fingers in the paints, some of them taste it, others smear their clothes. One of these many children tries on the big floppy black hat his father sometimes wears when he looks in the mirror and paints pictures of himself. It sinks down over his eyes. *Now I'm the artist!* he cries, blind to the world.

Then all is quiet; meaning now.

It's the time of day when shadow divides light, when things begin to take on weight and significance; common things like a spider hovering in a corner web. Like a stain on the floor, the shape of a cloud seen through the window. As though the world were telling a story, an ambiguous tale about betrayal. Now the wind dies down.

She stands before him by the window, holding a letter. *How much longer?*

Shh.

Tired. I'm tired.

Just a little longer.

The clock strikes. Her eye catches a glimpse of something red in the alleyway leading to the courtyard outside. She hears her husband's brush against the canvas, *hss.* She returns her look to the blank sheet of paper in her hand and parts her lips slightly, her mind lost in a maze of possibilities.

The artist likes to make up stories.

One day he himself will figure in a novel in which a character named Charles Swann is working in a desultory way on a study of the artist Jan Vermeer. He's working in a desultory way because he has both time on his hands and money. Actually he hasn't worked on it for years: it's become an excuse for him not to see a woman named Odette de Crécy, who has fallen for him and to whom, in turn, because she really doesn't appeal to him, he feels indifferent. At least at first.

She says, "You'll laugh at me, but this painter who keeps you from seeing me"—meaning the man who sits by the window, paint brush in hand, wondering—"I've never heard of him. Is he still alive? Can I see his paintings here in Paris, so I can at least see what you like, so I can understand what's going on inside that head of yours?"

Indifference turns to infatuation; then something like love. Her absences leave him troubled, his imagination wandering the city of Paris, dreaming up liaisons, the giddy laughter of an inconstant woman in the tapestried bedroom of another. He grows obsessed with Odette, who in truth has been kept by many men before him.

He begins to define her in terms of the women who appear in many of Botticelli's paintings: slim and angular; immobile, contemplating action. She becomes a figure fixed for posterity by an artist's brush; while the artist's works take on a peculiar life of their own, speaking in an intimate and personal manner to Charles Swann.

One evening she asks him if this Vermeer had ever been made to suffer by a woman, and if it was a woman who had inspired his work. When Swann replies that really very little is known about Vermeer, that one can only surmise, she loses all interest in the painter.

He grows jealous of Odette. He begins to suffer for her. He demands to know her whereabouts on the days and nights he is unable to see her, he asks her whom she's seen, how others look at her. He poses questions; she lies. His imagination soars. He pictures her with other men, even with other women. Evidence indicates a man named Forcheville has become her lover. He roams the avenues and boulevards of Paris, following her, spying on her, peering in windows and making inquiries; he aches for her when she's out of his sight.

Forcheville. The name grows in his mind like a tumor.

Then an odd thing happens: he begins to love her less. As though it had happened in another hemisphere, unnoticed by him, the comet of passion has burned itself out and fallen into the sea of indifference. And this woman, on whom, as he says, he has wasted so many years of his life, for whom he has experienced his greatest love, is not, in the end, even his type.

The story of Charles Swann and Odette de Crécy, in a nutshell.

I left something out. In the end he marries her. They have a daughter, Gilberte, on whom the narrator of the book, sometimes known, after his creator, as Marcel, had in his youth vainly invested *his* adoration. Afterwards this young man, an aspiring writer, directs his attentions to a young woman named Albertine, whom he meets on the beach at Balbec in Normandy. He grows intensely jealous of her, keeping her a virtual prisoner in his Paris apartment, interrogating her on her whereabouts, the liaisons he imagines for her, both male and female; until one day she escapes and dies in a riding accident.

In 1921 the man who wrote this novel, Marcel Proust, rose from his bed to attend an exhibition of the paintings of Vermeer of Delft, held at the Jeu de Paume. As he descended the stairs of his home in Paris he grew suddenly dizzy. He steadied himself and continued on, and though still not well he was steered through the exhibition by the art critic Jean-Louis Vaudoyer. He came to Vermeer's *View of Delft,* a scene the artist may have painted with the aid of a camera obscura, a convex lens set in a wall of a darkened room or box that projected on the opposite wall a view of the outside world, awaiting interpretation by the artist. Proust's

eye was caught by a detail, a section of wall splashed yellow with
sunlight. He stared at it for a while, then moved on, surviving the
night, the week, and dying eighteen months later.

Another character in his book (and a man Swann knew quite
well), the novelist Bergotte, has made his fortune by writing about
people in sitting rooms, wealthy people who move in the highest
society, who spend hours at the dinner table in scintillating
conversation.

Bergotte has been taken up by some of the best families. He
dines well, he has mistresses. His books have brought him much
money and renown.

But like his creator he is unwell. He suffers from insomnia;
when he sleeps at all he experiences nightmares. He's often overtaken by attacks of vertigo. There is pain. One day he experiences
a mild attack of uremia, yet he is determined to attend an exhibition
of the paintings of Vermeer: he especially wants to see his *View of
Delft.*

Though as he climbs the stairs of the gallery he feels suddenly
dizzy, he continues to make his way to the painting. As if he were
a child intent on catching a yellow butterfly that might at any
moment fly away, his eye is drawn to the right side of the painting,
where a fragment of wall is brilliantly lit by the sun. "That's how
I should have written," he says to himself. "My last books are too
dry. I should have added more layers of color, I should have made
every sentence as precious in itself as this little patch of yellow."
In a heavenly balance, a celestial scales, there appears to him,
weighing down one of the pans, his own life; while the other
contains the little patch of wall so exquisitely painted. Aware of
the gravity of his condition, he feels he has imprudently sacrificed
his life just to see the patch of yellow wall.

Mumbling to himself, "Little patch of yellow wall, little patch
of yellow wall," he sinks down on a chair, topples to the floor,
and dies.

One more thing: after Swann's death Odette does indeed marry Forcheville, the man with whom she had been betraying her husband. He adopts Odette's daughter Gilberte and gives her his name. It is as though Charles Swann had never existed.

The last word Proust wrote on his deathbed, on the back of an old envelope stained with tea, was *Forcheville*. And then, too weak to hold a pen, he called his housekeeper Céleste into his room and, feeling his life about to leave him, dictated a few last authentic details about the passing of the author Bergotte.

The artist turns his face away from the mirror.

The spider repairs its web.

The artist likes to make up stories.

A woman makes lace, and her portrait hangs in the Louvre. Eyes lowered, she remains oblivious to the faces and voices of those who stand watching her, the tourists and savants who fill the air with conjecture.

A pregnant woman standing before a painting of the Last Judgment holds an empty balance.

A woman reads a letter by an open window. Good news, or bad?

And is it really late afternoon?

The artist knows all the secrets.

Now the house is empty. In his mind's eye he sees it all: how she runs to meet him by the canal. In the tension of the afternoon she listens to the man's voice, the bubble and murmur of seduction. Her fingers slide along the bark of the tree. The air is broken by a sigh.

I love it when you do that.

The artist has an artist's temperament, he's easily roused to anger. In the long hours of his day he stews in jealousy as he sits mixing his colors, dipping his brush.

His wife is the first person to see his work. He sets his canvas on the easel, he awaits her comments. He watches her face, the twitching of an eyelid, the flaring of a nostril, tension in the mouth.

Look.

Every painting is a souvenir, an echo of a moment; a crystallization of suspicion; the beginning of knowledge.

Now he's painting a woman standing at a virginal. Her look of equanimity pierces the viewer as she fingers the keys. Daylight coming through the window behind her brilliantly catches the folds of her dress, the pearls around her neck, leaving much of her face in shadow. There's no trace of vulnerability here: this woman looks as if she's been let in on a secret. Maybe even *his* secret.

In a painting on the wall a cupid displays a playing card between his thumb and forefinger. He too looks outwards, directly at the viewer.

Read the signs, the woman and the cupid seem to be saying.

Open your eyes.

Look.

And the artist's wife turns away.

THREE SNAPSHOTS

I *saw you.*

I was barely awake. Words died in my throat.

I saw you. He told me the rest. And then he hung up, leaving me with the image of Marc Rougemont on his knees, the blade of the knife an inch away from his throat. That was how I re-membered I had left it: unfinished.

I tried to find the switch for the lamp and knocked the telephone to the floor and for a long moment the noise obliterated the quiet of the house.

"Who was it?"

"He said he was in New York. He said he saw me kill Marc Rougemont."

She sat up and touched my back. "But."

"I didn't kill him."

"What are you doing?"

"Trying to pick up the phone."

"Turn on the light."

"I can't find it."

"But who was it?"

"A man. A voice. I don't know." I switched on the lamp and Denise shut her eyes, turned abruptly away from it.

"It was my husband," she said.

"You can't be sure of that."

"Who else would it be?"

"But your husband doesn't know my number. He doesn't even know my name."

She said: "He knows everything." I thought of a man standing at a hotel window, watching, making deductions, waiting to pick up the phone.

I saw you.

"But you didn't kill him."

"No."

"I don't know what to believe."

"When I left he was on his knees, he was almost in tears. But he was alive." I looked at Denise.

"He's done this to me before," she said. "Phoned me in the middle of the night, asked me who I was with, what I was doing. He wouldn't lay a hand on you. It's me he's after."

I thought of the calls that came late at night after Kate had died, just after I'd returned from Italy. The blue Mercedes that had followed me from one town to the next, nearly as far as New Hampshire: it was as though time had been folded back on itself, like a bedsheet in the deft hands of a chambermaid.

Look.

Her eyes, beyond Marc's shoulder.

Denise in the cinema.

The ringing of a telephone just before dawn.

The car.

Eventually we drifted back into a fitful sleep, disturbed by dreams, awakened more than once by the creaks and noises of the house. We woke together at six and watched the sun rise, brilliant and yellow, until the snow became too painful to look at, dazzlingly white as it cloaked the trees and lay in drifts outside the house.

Denise was still in bed. I finished my coffee and put some more wood in the stove and went in to see her. She reached for me and drew me back beside her as she threw off the covers. I looked down at her in the light of morning, her pale skin. She stretched her arms above her head and, shutting her eyes, slowly parted her legs. This was our only defense, the potential for love. For a moment I savored the image before me, a woman lit by the sun. Then I pressed my lips to her breast.

‡　‡　‡

It arrived two days later: a plain white envelope with nothing on it but my name and address neatly typed on the front. Inside there were three photographs.

The first showed me under the awning of Marc's apartment house, the name "Vienna" clearly visible on it. The sidewalk was deserted. My hand was on the door handle and between the darkness of evening and the blaze of light from the lobby I was a silhouette: unmistakably me.

The second was hazy, the details blurred, but through the window I was holding something, undoubtedly the knife, and Marc was on his knees, his hands raised in the air as though at the climax of a sacrificial rite, a biblical scene painted long ago by an Old Master.

The last had been taken through the glass doors of Denise's hotel. We were standing by the elevator. Her hand was on my arm and I seemed to be staring directly into the lens of the camera. Moments later the doors would open and we would be on our way to her room. Afterwards anything could have happened, the story was up to the viewer. But then the phone would ring.

Go.

Now.

I tried to call Marc and was momentarily relieved when the ringing stopped and I heard his voice. But it was only the tape on his answering machine, apologizing for his absence, requesting a message, alleging he would get back to me as soon as possible. I remembered he had gone to Paris for a few weeks. I tried to think of him as my victim, his body shuddering as the blood poured from his throat, staining the carpet red, like a map being swiftly unrolled across a floor.

"What does he want from me?"

She said nothing.

"Money? The man drives a Mercedes, what more could he need?"

"It's not money he wants. It's like a game to him. He'll try to destroy you."

"This is his idea of fun? Couldn't he play golf like other judges?"

"He knows how you're taking this, he's trying to unnerve you."

"And how long will he go on with it? Until I break?"

"Or I return to him."

And then it would start all over again.

Denise stayed with me until Thursday. She called the bank and told them she was too ill to go back to work before the end of the week, when she was scheduled to fly to New York to see a client. How long would it be before her husband, who to me was merely a memory of a half-noticed face in a restaurant, a looming presence in a darkened cinema, his raised arm bisecting the screen, how long before he drove up to confront us?

We could have left, of course, we could have driven to Vermont or even Canada. We could have taken a flight out of Boston, to London or Paris or Singapore. And yet it seemed to me that no matter where we went the net merely would have widened, enclosed the world not because the judge had connections but because we were all linked together by a web of circumstance that had begun with a few exchanged looks, eyes meeting eyes.

The heat of the sun had begun to melt the snow. The roads were clear. I stood by the living-room window watching drips of water fall steadily from the roof. A woman rode her horse along the edge of the road, slowly, cautiously, the hollow sound of its hooves as it walked breaking the silence. Her breath condensing in the air, her body moving languidly in the saddle, she turned briefly to me, oblivious to what was happening to us and yet now another small element in it.

I thought of my novels, all of them set in the summer, during the interminable hours and days of a heat wave. Shadows leaned out of darkened doorways, people disappeared, others went mad in a city of strangers, moving through a landscape full of bewilderment, indecipherable signs; in the grip of something inevitable. I'd always thought such things were impossible in the clarity of autumn, the freshness of spring, the slippery brilliance of winter. But I'd forgotten that at night everything turned to ice. Now her husband's arrival seemed to me inevitable, imminent.

Half to myself I said, "You want me to kill him, don't you. You want him to come up here and you want me to do it then. Because there doesn't seem like there's anything left to do."

She said nothing.

"You won't let me call the police."

"I told you, they won't believe you."

I looked at her. "So what is it?"

"I never said you had to kill him."

"You want me to do it for you. You want him out of the way and you want me to do it. Just say it."

"No."

"Go on. Say it. Say that you want me to kill him."

"No, David," and she laughed a little uneasily, as if this were a game whose rules were not quite clear to her.

"Just say it out loud. It's what you've been thinking, isn't it, it's what you've been hinting at. You just want me to come to that conclusion."

"Don't be ridiculous."

"Say it. Say 'Kill my husband.' "

"Stop it."

"Use the words, put them together, for God's sake just say it yourself."

"I won't listen to you."

"Then put it another way, say 'I wish he were dead.' Go ahead, say it, let it out."

She turned to me. Quietly she said, "You almost killed Marc Rougemont. You admitted it yourself."

"But I didn't. I couldn't."

"Only because it wouldn't have made any difference, it wouldn't have brought Kate back to you. If it could have, you would have done it."

"But think of it. If it happened, if I did what you wanted me to do, I'd be a murderer."

"Accidents happen. People become careless. It's just the way things are."

An accident. Kate standing on the subway platform. *She must have lost her footing,* Josie had told me that morning.

Marc's words came back to me: *It's your fault she died.*

Denise looked at me, she held my face between her hands and looked me in the eyes. "You know that I'm falling in love with you, David."

I felt a chill come over me, I pulled away from her. "What if I'm caught? What if the police find me? What if I go to jail?"

"Don't think about it."

"I'm a writer, not a murderer. I teach English. I grade essays, I discuss metaphors. When I write I start chapters, I end them. I

invent plots, I create characters." Just like Marc Rougemont, I
thought.

"And you kill them off, just as you did in your last novel."

"It's different. It's easier. Sometimes they just disappear."

"Do this for me. For us."

"Sometimes I don't even bother finding them. They just go.
They walk out, merge with the crowd, slip into thin air. They live
on paper, they can be erased."

"It's for us," she repeated.

Oh yes. I too was falling in love, reducing the distance between
us. And yet simultaneously I was beginning to look at her from a
different angle. What was this all about? Is this why I had been
brought into it, to fulfill her plan? And had Kate and Marc had
similar conversations?

I want him out of the way.

He's making life impossible for me.

‡   ‡   ‡

The artist likes to make up stories.

A PLOT

What if.

What if the artist himself has sent her the letter.

What if the artist has sent her more than one letter. All forgeries.

Meet me.

What if the artist has in some perverse way involved his wife in some imaginary intrigue, some devious, complex network of possibilities. Just to see her reactions. Curiosity. Pleasure. Infatuation. Fear. Disappointment. Those brief unguarded moments of imbalance.

Eyes down.

Pretend you're reading.

Bad news.

Shh.

What if the artist has done this because he needs to see his wife—his model—try on, so to speak, all the various emotions of a quiet life in Delft. Like the surface of water this life can be disturbed, rippled, agitated.

She receives letters. *I love you.*
I want you.
Meet me.

But what if she actually does have an admirer, a flesh-and-blood admirer, who with her complicity has taken advantage of the artist's ruse, his little game? Plot, counterplot.

Is he the man in the red jacket whom she has seen once or twice before, in fact more than once or twice, during the course of their days, her long afternoon walks when the artist is busy at work filling in the colors, adding details, when the artist requires peace and quiet?

I love you.
I desire you.
Meet me.

A red jacket becomes a pronoun; then a detail in her life. Her imagination begins to build upon it. She can see the two of them walking along the canal, she hears his words in her ear, she can almost feel his touch, and suddenly out of a speck of color seen from a window a whole future begins to blossom, words, looks, caresses.

Late afternoon. The house is empty, the artist has stepped out to buy paints, more of that red, to complete the jacket on the man about to pay the procuress. Sunlight strikes the floor near the chair. A broom leans in the corner. He gazes down at her in the bedroom. *Yes oh yes.*

What if.

One day the artist comes upon her in the kitchen. It's a bit early for a drink, yet she's dipped into the wine and she's fallen into a stupor. She's been drinking because she's not been quite herself lately. It's an odd thing: sometimes she's the artist's wife and the mother of their children. At other times she feels pulled in four different directions. She sometimes imagines herself leaving

Delft, carrying her few possessions in a bag, increasing her speed, taking flight.

She sees herself growing old in the little house filled with paintings, those that are finished and others that retain only an outline, the beginnings of a face, the hint of a reflection. As though in capturing at different times her separate emotions he were creating a kind of puzzle. Put them together and he might possess her wholly.

The artist stands and watches her, sometimes with both his eyes, other times out of the corner of one, and sometimes even with the aid of a mirror.

Darkness is beginning to fall and she's dreaming. In her dream the man in the red jacket is standing by the elm tree. He raises an eyebrow, touches the side of his cheek, sets his jaw. She's only ever seen him from a distance, from the window where she stands holding a letter.

Eyes down.

Pretend you're reading.

Now at last she feels his breath on her face, his eyes fixing hers. She turns back to look at her house. All the windows are closed. All but one. He lowers his eyes to her bosom, imagining what she will look like undressed, on the bed beneath the rise and fall of his lean body; and because this comes easily to him, he, too, considers himself an artist. Everybody in Delft is an artist: the husband, the lacemaker, the wife and the lover, each creating the other.

Now anything is possible. Her hand is on the bark of the tree, her hand is suddenly overtaken and enclosed by the warmth of his.

Not now.

He takes her hand and draws her away from the canal, from the tree, towards the houses. *When I was in the war,* he begins, and his voice is lost as the wind rises, as the voices of others, those who take their afternoon stroll, those who are drunk, spinning on their heels by the edge of a canal, the children as they shout and laugh on their way back from school, the police spies, master artists of disguise, pretending to be you or me or him or simply another, they drown out everything but the heat of her thoughts.

Late afternoon. A bedroom, the door ajar. A broom, waning autumn sunlight on the chessboard floor.

Yes oh yes.

The man in the red jacket finds her husband pitiable. Just think: he paints those pictures, then drags them around from baker to butcher to candlestick maker, hoping to trade the woman putting on her necklace for a fresh loaf or a fat ham.

He thinks of his hand exploring the curve of her thigh, investigating the warm damp cleft that separates it from its mate. Time is passing.

Yes oh yes.

Shh.

She thinks of her husband by the open window, painting a picture of a woman making lace.

This is what she is thinking as they walk away from the canal.

They go to a tavern far from her home where her husband sits by an open window, painting, looking, considering things; and this image lingers in her mind like the phantom of one long dead.

The man in the red jacket introduces her to his friend, a musical gentleman. *Ta-dee dalaa.*

The man in red buys her a drink.

Have another.

She has another.

He speaks under his breath. *Now. It must be.*

He stands behind her and presses his hand to her left breast, gauges the width and weight of it, discreetly inspects it with the joints of his fingers. What will he give her in return, how will this transaction be played out? The trappings of love, the counterfeit promises: a metaphorical coin.

Now she will rise and go with him.

Now she wakes up, and when she opens her eyes she sees her husband standing in the doorway, watching her, taking her in. He holds a pair of scales in his hand. His black hat is on his head. Now he is ready to paint.

And when she holds the balance, watches it carefully, is she seeing something other than pearls and gold on the empty pans of the scales?

THE JUDGE

The call came just after seven that evening.

I was on my way out to a faculty meeting at the college, my first since taking a leave of absence. The spring semester was due to start in mid-January. I had been slated to teach my usual two courses, Introduction to Literature, The Art of the Novel. The meetings were unavoidable: if you missed even one, mildly abusive notes, typed on an IBM electric, were slipped anonymously in your mailbox.

A quarterly ritual, it was enacted in the overheated basement library, the air filled with requests and complaints buried in the polite verbiage of academia. A collection would be taken and Chinese food brought in from a restaurant in town resembling a huge antique junk becalmed in a parking lot. Copies of the agenda, minutes from the last meeting, people's notes, would quickly be covered with grease. Ribs stripped of meat became an ossuary on a sheet of newspaper; the odor of sweet-and-sour pork and fried rice mingled with the stink of turpentine and cigarette smoke. No disillusion here: I had always imagined an art school somehow resembling an artist's studio: serious work in the midst of chaos and dust.

I looked forward to the meeting. I hadn't been able to write since Kate's death, I needed to get back into my old routine, my old life, and yet a new life, alone, productive, serene. Teaching meant leaving the house three mornings a week, returning to write late in the afternoon: I had grown used to it, my fingers tapping out stories of people haunted by their pasts, people who vanish, those caught in the obsession of loss, fearful of death. Afternoon would shade to evening, night would fall, darkness punctuated by the cry of the owl. I had been living too long in a world that seemed to defy comprehension, that could not be mastered: the shadows, the deceit, the uncertainty.

And then Denise had come into my life, and because I was no longer alone solitude reappeared like a third party, something malign and brooding, an unwanted guest in the house. Her very presence implied absence.

She was in the kitchen making dinner for herself. Having spent so long going from one hotel to another, flying off to this meeting and that, she seemed to delight in the prosaic world of my little house. Yet every time the phone rang, time stopped, silence fell.

Our eyes met.

He said, "Mr. Reid?"

I listened. Denise stared at me.

"I'm sure you've already received the photographs. It's only a matter of time before the police find him."

"What do you want?"

"Maybe even at this moment a neighbor is complaining of the smell."

"Just tell me."

For a few moments he said nothing. Then: "I've already got what I want."

"Not money."

"I don't need money."

"I don't have money. So what is it?"

"I've got you just where I want you. Right in the picture."

"You were following Marc. You took a room in the same hotel I was in." It was like telling an old story, one he'd heard a thousand times before.

"Don't be so stupid. I don't care about the Frenchman, he's nothing to me. I was watching you. I've known about you a long time. You and my wife."

"But."

"And now I want her back."

"I never killed Marc. I just wanted to talk to him. He'd been having an affair with my wife, she killed herself because of him."

Denise was about to say something and I put my finger to my lips.

"Then you understand exactly how I feel," and the judge paused, waiting for me to see it all as clearly as he did.

"He's gone to Paris," I said. "He flew off the next morning."

"You're sure of that."

"It's what he told me."

"You mean he told you what he was going to do. Come on, Mr. Reid, that's not the same as what he did."

"I know that I never killed him."

"Do you know his phone number in Paris? Can you actually prove that he went, have you called the airlines, checked with his publishers?"

"I don't need to. I told you, I never touched him."

"Maybe a plea of insanity will save you."

It dawned on me: Denise's husband had killed him.

"So what happens now?"

He laughed to himself. "That's up to you, my friend. You can leave my wife, we can forget about the Frenchman, walk away from it all. Or I can go to people I know in the police and show them the photograph."

"Which isn't proof that I did it."

"There are fingerprints," he said. "Once they see the photo they'll put two and two together. Otherwise I can destroy the negative and forget your name and your fingerprints will mean nothing at all to them."

"And undoubtedly you wore gloves."

"I had nothing to do with this, Mr. Reid. I simply witnessed it. I've witnessed a great many things over the past few years, you know."

"How do you know she's even here with me?"

"But I can see her standing there, watching you. Did I get you out of bed, Mr. Reid? Were you and Denise under the covers, were you fucking her?"

I said nothing.

"She's good, isn't she. She's a good lover, my wife. She knows all the moves, she knows just what to say, what to do. And she's a beautiful woman. But she's my wife."

"So what's the deal? I give up Denise and you go back to beating her?"

"Why don't you ask her yourself?" he said, putting down the receiver.

Of course he was right: it was still only a matter of time before the police began to question all of Marc's contacts, to track down the names and addresses in his little black book, the countless blondes, the editors and friends. A photographer would capture the scene of the crime from every angle: the body on the floor, its arm outstretched; the blood-soaked fibers of the rug; the knife. Fingerprints would be taken as a matter of course: I could see them rolling onto the page from my inky fingers, I could hear the noise of the police station, the earthy jibes, the clacking of a typewriter, the laughter of the fat detective as he read the morning paper; the radio, a murmur of music and traffic reports, tie-ups on the Brooklyn-Queens Expressway. I would be kept waiting on a wooden bench in a waiting room. The radiator would hiss and startle; figures would move beyond the glass partition: the fat detective, the duty officer, the nervous gestures of a man in shirtsleeves and dark glasses, his Smith & Wesson in its holster. Then the small talk would end. Someone would compare the prints with a jeweler's glass, or project them side by side onto a screen. I would be taken to another room to be questioned by two men. Barred windows. Graffiti on the walls: *Joe Loves Cathy; Cops Suck; Tell It to the Judge.* The pungent terrified smell of spilled urine.

The smarmy preliminaries: smiles and chitchat. Then the questions, the demand for details: where were you when, what time did you, how did you.

Never *why*. Tell *that* to the judge.

There would be a lineup: beyond the two-way mirror Denise's husband watching, scrutinizing. *Definitely the one on the left,* I could hear him whispering, *the small dark-haired man, the one with the bewildered smile.*

I wondered if I should call a lawyer, try to explain things as calmly and clearly as possible, relate a story about a jealous husband and his beautiful wife, a tale of revenge and entrapment that seemed to have everything but a beginning. The phone calls. The Mercedes that followed me. Nothing made any sense when you went back that far.

There was little I could do but go to the meeting at the college. As though it were so easy to walk out of one story back into another.

‡   ‡   ‡

It went on for almost three hours. Previous minutes were approved, the dean's report delivered. Sabbaticals were requested.

The chairman of the long-range planning committee spoke lengthily of the future. The professor of printmaking picked quietly through his lo mein. I was treated by my colleagues as though nothing at all had happened: Kate had become a shadow buried under layers of paint, in its place a quiet domestic scene: a chair, a table, a painting on the wall.

When had this all begun, where were its origins? In that expression on Kate's face that last evening I saw her? Was I meant to have read the truth in it, followed the thread of her fear into the future I was now trapped in? Or was it something I had done, or said, something I had overlooked, that could have been prevented? Denise had come with her husband to the restaurant where I was having lunch with Marc. She'd followed me to the cinema and then was struck to the floor by her husband. Marc was dead; or he was in Paris. I was caught in a web of doubt, of words on a telephone, and I thought of Kate reading the letter that last afternoon: sentences on a page knotting themselves into an inescapable plot; a plot either Marc or I could have invented, imposed upon our hapless characters. The judge had me just where he wanted me. But who was framing whom?

When I returned home at ten thirty Denise was waiting up for me. She had locked and bolted the front door and drawn all the curtains. There had been no further calls from her husband.

She sat at the kitchen table, smoking a cigarette. She had just showered and was wearing my old bathrobe, a tattered silk thing that had once belonged to my father. She lifted her face to kiss me and placed my hand on her breast and the smoke hung between us in the still air.

"He's going to pin Marc's death on me unless you go back to him."

She shook her head. "I can't do that. I won't."

Suddenly she saw the choice: me or him. Or rather the choice was mine: Denise or nothing.

But there weren't any choices.

I said, "I want you, Denise. I can't let you go. I can't lose you."

What would happen to us? Would we always be on the run, fugitives from law, like characters in a film? Or could this be brought to a sudden and satisfactory conclusion?

It would be an accident.

Then what?

The plot hung in the air, a mist of an idea begging for shape and recognition, like something conjured up at a seance, a shade surviving in both the past and the future, awaiting the inevitable questions.

A man slipping beneath the wheels of a subway train.

A man tumbling from a hotel window.

She said, "It doesn't have to happen here. It'll be easier in the city."

"It's crazy."

"Nobody will ever know."

"What if Marc isn't dead, what if your husband's only bluffing?"

"It doesn't change anything," she said. "He's still my husband. He'll never let me go."

Her face betrayed nothing as she wove the strands together. "I'll phone him tomorrow from the airport. I'll tell him I'm leaving him, filing for divorce."

"And then you're going to New York."

"That's right."

"When's your meeting?"

"Saturday morning. Early. So I have to be there Friday night. Come down on a separate flight. We'll stay in the same hotels we were in before."

"He'll follow you."

"That's what we want him to do, isn't it?"

Three lines that would converge on a dark street or subway platform in Manhattan sometime in the next thirty-six hours.

She had nothing more to say. The hours that followed were filled with silence. The future was up to me. I found my mind slipping into a calm, murderous mode; I wondered if we could arrange to have her husband killed, if Denise had underworld contacts, if she had liquid assets, say ten or twenty thousand, enough to pay a hit man, and I could see him walking away from the hotel room, the body on the floor, the blood on the walls, boarding a plane for El Paso and disappearing from our lives forever.

Until the day he loosened his lips. In a saloon, as the tumbleweed rolled across the plain in an endless whisper. In a state penitentiary against a chorus of banging cell doors. This too would hang over our lives.

An accident.

At midnight she began to get ready for bed. From the bathroom door I watched as she washed her face, applied lotions. I watched as she undressed and got into bed. I imagined the house empty, my life without her, and it was as though she were compelling me to see my life once again diminished. Here she was beside me; in another day or two she would be gone, very likely forever. A repeat of Kate's disappearance.

How long could it go on? Denise would haunt me, a possibility somewhere in the world, in New York or Hong Kong or Boston, waiting for someone else who would save her from her husband the judge. My imagination would begin to build upon her, I would see her with other men, in other cities, my mind displaying one picture after another of this woman who had vanished from my life forever. Could I afford to let her go? Or could I this time show the courage I had always lacked and take control of my life, pull the strings the way I wanted them, arrange the chapters in just the right order?

She lay back on the pillow and looked at me, and parting her lips seemed to smile.

28

FILM NOIR

The artist knows all the secrets.

No.

The artist knows only that he does not know.

Perhaps the artist is incapable of further knowledge. Once the proverbial fly on the wall, he's strayed into the web, he can see the spider patiently eyeing him, fidgety and spindly. He can see the web, he can describe it, but he's inside it: trapped, unable to escape, unaware of the dimensions of his predicament. Uninvolved until it's too late.

Is it possible that he paints only what he sees, and later, when sitting in his studio, looking over the canvases leaning against the walls, propped on old easels, hanging from the odd nail, he begins to discern something else emerging from them?

Patterns are formed; plots acquire outlines. Unspoken words linger in the air.

On a shelf in the artist's studio is a book by the Flemish artist Jan Vredeman de Vries, who published his influential study on perspective in 1604–5. In it is a drawing by the author: a room whose walls, ceiling, and floor are divided into equal segments, precisely distorted by the presumed line of sight, as though each plane were a chessboard. On the floor, stretching away from us, a body lies with one arm extended to the side. Entering the room at the rear is a man with his left arm raised. He seems about to say something, to cry out; or perhaps he's calling out the name of the man who lies lifeless on the floor. Hidden behind a half-open door at the side is another man, a smiling man. They're all linked by a series of lines generating from the eye of the man entering with his arm raised. Each of the men is simultaneously caught by our gaze, trapped within a network of sight lines, the geometry of vision. Unlike the man entering the room we, and the artist, can see it all: the man on the floor, the man behind the door, that man pushing his way in. The vanishing point is located at the intruder's eyes, in his brain. It is a vast web in which all three are snared the moment the scene is reflected in our eyes. As elaborate as a piece of lace. Or a chord struck on a lute.

The artist knows the picture well: and because he lives in a world of images, because his memory is a series of portraits and landscapes, sketches and diagrams, it comes back to him once again. He thinks about what he doesn't see when he looks at the picture, about what he can't see. His mind can only provide the details, add the colors, shed light on it; he can even speculate on the sequel to the picture. Will there be a battle, a duel, will the room suddenly be filled with action, sight lines pulling this way and that over and around the lifeless body on the floor, as though this were a trio of marionettes attached to strings?

Or will the murderer remain hidden behind his door, watching the innocent man kneel over the corpse, leaving traces of himself, absorbing the guilt that fills the room?

Checkmate.

But the artist thinks only about seeing.

He has used the vanishing point to skillful effect.

An officer and a girl are sitting at a table by the same open window in which her face had been darkly reflected, shattered into four, as she read the letter.

Now the light streams in, falls squarely on the laughing face of the young woman, on the wall behind her, the map that hangs on it. Sitting across from her is a man in a red jacket, his black hat still on his head. We can't see his face; or rather we can make out only the shape of his nose, a dark slit of an eye. His right hand rests on his hip, the fingers curled towards us. Is this the man in the red jacket we've seen so much of lately? Or is it someone else, his predecessor perhaps; or maybe even an idealized version of him, some actor in her dreams, a man who might have been?

If only.

The woman, wearing a white head-scarf and holding a glass of wine, is laughing. Was it something he said? Has he made a proposal, and is she laughing because her mind is clear, she is free to do as she wishes? *This is how things should be,* she thinks.

The artist knows how to use the vanishing point, he plays with our perceptions. Here he locates it midway between the young woman and the man, so that our eye is drawn to a stretch of blank wall. What can we see there when we look? Are we in some abstract way aware of the bond between these two people, are our eyes tugged in this direction and that, do they shift nervously as though teetering on the brink of something between the officer whose dark figure looms in the foreground, the woman whose smiling face is so brightly illuminated by sunlight? Or is the space between them like a screen on which we can project scenes from a life, past, present, and future?

Let's sit back and watch.

There's a woman weighing pearls and gold.

And look, there she is again, putting on her strand of pearls.

Here she is once more, sitting at a table, drunk, asleep, presumably dreaming.

Fragments of an identical world . . . the same table, the same carpet, the same woman, as Proust once observed.

Not much of a film. Not until we ourselves begin to fill in the spaces between these scenes. You see, before light can be perceived there must be darkness.

29

VANISHING POINT

I saw him again when I came down from Denise's room and the elevator door opened. I imagined he was waiting for her. Undoubtedly he had been there for most of the day.

There was a convention in town and the lobby, a bright spacious area broken up by columns and love seats, was crowded with insurance agents. Odd man out: I seemed to be the only one there not wearing a business suit and lapel badge, the one person without a look of cheerful urgency smeared in panic across his face. Save for the judge, like a figure in a painting, his intentions still a mystery.

He was standing by the newsstand, our looks briefly crossing as I walked towards the door and out into the afternoon. I pretended not to recognize him, I couldn't afford to be drawn into his world, the appalling logic of his mind. He seemed younger than when I'd seen him that first time in the restaurant, afterwards raising his arm to strike his wife to the ground. He had a pleasant, open face, and I could see it distorting with jealousy and anger at those moments when Denise came to mind, when she was out of his sight, beyond the limits of knowledge. And I could imagine him sitting on the bench in his judicial capacity, berobed and solemn, patiently addressing the injured party, offering lollipops to a child at a custody hearing in his chambers. What went through his mind at such moments, during the long hours of a divorce case, the testimony he had heard countless times before, the brutality, the irreconcilable differences, the loss of faith? Was there a central image surrounded by a symmetry of speculation, his wife trapped in the sticky complications of infidelity: Denise in bed with this man or that; the bleak interiors of air terminals as she traveled from Boston to L.A., to London and Paris and Geneva, to Tokyo and Hong Kong, each time meeting someone else, making love, whispering about the husband she had left behind?

But now there was a difference. Now he had a name on which to attach his suspicions. A name and a face, a definition.

I stopped at the window of the shop that sold antique optical instruments. The display had been altered, the painting of the man and the globe had been taken away and the telescopes and astrolabes and sextants replaced by old microscopes, some of which were engraved with the names of their makers, the dates of manufacture, 1675, 1789: elaborate script pressed long ago into the polished brass tubes. I wondered if this was a seasonal ritual, something to do with Christmas or New Year's Eve, the owner of the shop encouraging his customers to examine the molecules and parasites of life, the hydras and amoebas and minutiae, the tiny worlds within a drop of blood, the infernal mindless struggles in a universe of pond water, the frantic homunculi in a puddle of sperm, rather than the murky atmospheres and glowing rings of distant planets.

When the woman who worked the desk at my hotel saw me return she stepped out from her little office. The television was on and a man said, *This lady claims to be possessed by the spirit of*

Anko. The woman smiled and asked me if my room was all right.

"Of course it is."

"I didn't want to say anything before. When you checked in, I mean. Because of the lady. You know what I mean."

"Everything's fine," I said, trying not to betray my unease.

"There were no calls, no visitors?"

"No," she said, "nothing," and her eyes moved slowly back and forth across my face as though trying to decipher a code, something written in another language. "She's been on the phone, your wife. But nothing came in for you. I bet it's cold as hell in Boston."

"It's pretty bitter."

"So far we've been lucky." She paused. "It's funny, this season. It's different. The greenhouse effect, I guess. They talk about it on television. Things aren't like they used to be. So. Your room is okay? You don't want to move this time?"

"Not this time."

"You travel to New York a lot?"

"Sometimes."

"Business, I guess," and I said that she was absolutely right, I often had to come to New York on business. She slid a cigarette from a pack and tapped it on the counter. "What do you do?"

I didn't know what to say, and so for a few moments the two of us stood in a shared silence, gazing at each other. "Anyway it's none of my business," she said.

When I returned to my room Denise was standing by the window, smoking a cigarette, still dressed in the trim blue suit she'd worn at the meeting earlier that day in a suite at the Pierre. All had gone smoothly: this time there had been no interference from her husband. Portfolios had been reviewed and updated, papers signed. I stood behind her and rested my hands on her waist. I could smell her hair, the spray of scent she had applied to her throat. In three years I'd be doing this; in ten, in twelve. We'd have a house somewhere, with a circular drive. Would we have forgotten all of this by then, the schemes, the body lying in the roadway?

I pressed my lips to the back of her neck. She said: "He still thinks I'm in my room." She laughed a little. "I've left instructions at the desk not to put any calls through to me. My husband has no way of knowing whether I'm there or not."

I could still see him that last time I was in the city, a little over a week before, standing across the street in front of Marc's building, chatting with the doorman of the Vienna, sharing a laugh, the two men throwing their heads back and baring their teeth. The judge lightly touching the other's back in a gesture of fellowship.

I saw you.

She looked at her watch. "He's supposed to meet me at eight. Three hours left." She turned to me. "I'm exhausted."

It had been cloudy all day and now the darkness of late afternoon was beginning to fall over the city, a threat of snow hanging acidly in the air. Still the curtains on Marc's window were tightly shut. In other apartments life went on: a woman was setting a table for dinner; another stood talking on the telephone, smoking a cigarette; a man sat at his desk typing. I had tried to call Marc earlier and again reached only his answering machine: it was impossible to know whether he was on the floor, decaying and stinking the place out, or at that moment eating canard à l'orange at La Tour d'Argent. I could assume either, or neither. Or, I now sometimes think, both.

"Did you make those calls?"

She looked at me. "His publisher in Paris hasn't seen him. But he hadn't a specific appointment with him. He said that the last he'd heard from Marc was that he'd intended to come to Paris, but he also was going to Rome. He didn't know his itinerary. And the airline wouldn't release any information to me. Something about the legality of it, especially involving a flight that took place over a week earlier."

"Did you say you were Marc's wife?"

"I tried that. They wouldn't tell me anything. And I phoned his apartment in Paris. No answer." She said, "I'm tired, David." Her voice was distant, as though she were speaking to me from another room.

"Try to get some sleep," I said.

She looked at me. "You know what to do?"

We'd been over it fifty times.

"He'll be on the corner, waiting for me. We'll meet an hour later. You rented the van?"

It was a small, privately owned outfit in Washington Heights: no questions asked, cash only, pay in advance. The man sat behind a battered desk covered with bills, old newspapers, a paper cup half-filled with coffee, the remains of a hamburger. A transistor radio with the stub of an aerial wrapped in foil played Latin music, conga drums and frenzied maracas, all the gaiety of an underpopulated border town at festival time. He said, "Leave it out there when you're done." It was an old battered Ford with a spotlight attached to the roof, bent uselessly over. When I told him I needed it to move my stuff to a new apartment he seemed not to hear. His ears were filled with fictions.

The engine started on the third try. I sat and waited for it to warm up. The street was familiar to me, its identity utterly changed. Once it had been filled with grocers, kosher butchers, dry cleaners. There had been a toy shop run by a man with a number tattooed on his forearm, where my mother used to take me before we'd visit my grandmother, a gift of appeasement, something to keep me busy while they drank borscht and argued in the kitchen. Old Russians used to walk past us on their way to the park to play chess or read their newspapers. Now the people were younger, they spoke a different language. Something of my past erased forever: where had it gone?

The traffic that Saturday was heavy. Christmas was only two

weeks away. There was something frantic in the air. I had parked the van in a lot around the corner from Marc's building, then walked up to Denise's hotel to get her suitcase. It was when I came down that I had seen the judge.

"You don't like it, do you."

I looked at her. I shook my head. She'd read my mind.

"It'll be an accident," she said. "Only an accident. Wait at the end of the street until he starts to follow me across."

"I can't do it," I said. "It's impossible."

"Nothing's impossible."

"This is."

"He doesn't matter to you. Think of us. Think of how it'll be. We'll get an apartment in Boston, we'll live together. Maybe even marry." She smiled wanly. "Just think. Just remember. An accident, not murder."

"But we'll know differently, won't we." The complications began to pile up in my mind. Denise and I would be linked by the knowledge of what we had done, by the guilt, the fact that each could place the blame on the other, and this stalemate would somehow unite us in mutual silence.

She touched my cheek with her hand and kissed me softly on the lips. "Go," she said. "Get something to eat. I'm not hungry."

Neither was I, but I couldn't sit still, I couldn't keep calm. I went out for a walk. Santa was on every other corner, ringing his bell, collecting money for the homeless and the hungry, and sometimes there were Salvation Army bands, uniformed men and women blowing trumpets and banging tambourines in the terrible cold of the afternoon, the air thick with Christmas carols and strained holiday cheer.

I hadn't any appetite. Later, when it was all over, I would be ravenous, I could see us in a restaurant tossing back the champagne, devouring our blackened tuna, in a celebratory mood.

When I returned at six thirty she was asleep, the covers pulled

to her chin, the curled fingers of a hand by her mouth: the
innocence of childhood making one last appearance. Her breathing
was light and regular. Her nerves were on edge: a decade of
marriage, of escape and evasion, had worn her down. Now that
it was about to come to an end she felt at ease, in balance, able
to sink into unguarded sleep. I decided against waking her until
it was time to go. In little over half an hour Denise would leave
and he would be waiting for her at a corner in the labyrinth of
deserted streets near the docks, and I had rehearsed the ensuing
events so often in my mind that it was as though it had already
been done, I could see him on the sidewalk, in the street, I could
hear the impact, he would go hurtling through the air, I could
imagine him lying crumpled and damaged on the road.

A face in a restaurant.

A woman struck from her cinema seat.

The phone call a few days later. *I'd like to see you again.*

Marc. Kate.

And for one brief moment the truth of what was happening
struck me like a piece of litter, a scrap of newspaper propelled by
the gritty breezes that blew up out of nowhere between the sky-
scrapers, attaching itself to my leg, flying off into the distance.

I sat and watched her sleep, not so much waiting for her to
rouse, to turn and stretch and open an exploratory eye, but rather
to read the signs in her face, the frowns and smiles, the creasing
of her brow. Occasionally a tiny noise would come from the bed,
a whimper or a stifled cry, as though she were trapped within a
dream, the intersecting lines of unconscious thought and association
pulling her this way and that. These were matters for speculation.

Dreams about her husband.

Dreams about me.

About *him.*

The plot grew thick with pronouns.

I found the letter in her briefcase while she slept. I'm not sure what I had been looking for. Perhaps I knew it all along. Or maybe I had lost my ability to trust anyone, and searching for evidence fell upon it, as though to fulfill some twist in the plot. The envelope was identical to the one in Kate's drawer, the handwriting the same: only the address differed, a post office box in Boston. It was written on blue paper and had been mailed a week earlier from New York. And I wondered if Denise had also stood by a window, gripping the page tightly between her hands, her expression unreadable.

He spoke of how much he missed her, how at night he yearned for her, desired to make love to her, and I imagined her weighing possibilities, measuring the tensions of her life. I looked across at the black rectangle of his window. The world was a mesh of doubt and uncertainty, my role in it still unknown to me.

When she woke she found me sitting beside her on the bed, and she reached for me, she passed her hand through my hair. I switched on the bedside lamp. "When," I began to say, and she placed her fingers against my lips, as though she knew my question in advance.

"I was dreaming about you. I dreamed we were making love."

"Any good?"

She smiled. "It was delicious."

"As good as with the others?"

"There aren't any others."

"Not one?"

"No," she said, pulling me down to her.

‡   ‡   ‡

At first I said nothing about the letter. I attempted to interpret her gestures and expressions, her responses to me; measuring the space between us. She dressed and put on her coat and got ready to leave. I watched as she brushed her hair before the mirror on the wall. I had nothing left to lose. I said, "How long have you known Marc Rougemont?"

She stopped and stared at my reflection.

"How long?"

Calmly she said, "Almost two years. I met him in Paris when I was there on business. It was one of the reasons he came to New York."

"You knew him before he met Kate."

She walked to the window. "I saw your wife once. Walking out of his apartment house," and she lifted her chin towards the building across the way. "She was with Marc, they'd probably just made love. I was very jealous of her."

I remembered that night I waited in my hotel room, preparing to confront Marc, I recalled the woman in his flat, how much like Denise she was, how she resembled Kate. He'd told me she was just a friend, an editor from Paris. Was her disappointing meeting with a client, sabotaged by her husband, also a fiction, a lie?

"He never told you about my wife, then?"

"I told you, I saw them coming out of his building. That's how I found out about her. I was going to surprise him. This has nothing to do with you and me. My husband knew nothing about him. I'm finished with Marc, anyway, it's all over."

"So your husband was lying. Marc's not dead," and as the weight and tensions of the past week lifted from me I felt almost giddy. "Then where the hell is he?"

She paused for a moment. "It doesn't matter now, does it."

"You knew all along he was alive. That phone call from your husband. You let him play with me."

"We'd better go, David. He's expecting me at eight. You know what to do."

"But why? Why did you do this?"

"So you could see for yourself what my husband's like."

"You never thought I would kill him just for you."

"I didn't know, David. I just," and she fell silent.

I took hold of her arm and pulled her gently towards me. "Did Marc ever speak of Kate?"

"I asked him about her. He didn't deny it. He told me who she was, that she was married to a writer like himself. I knew who you were, I knew your name. He told me he had got her pregnant." She said, "You knew that, didn't you."

"I suspected it."

"I think he enjoyed it, having two women. Maybe there were more. There's a woman in Paris he'd also been seeing, a journalist I think. He liked the idea of the intrigue, the deceptions." She shrugged. "The plots and subplots."

"But not the pregnancy."

"That worried him," she said. "She wanted to have the baby."

"Then she would have had to tell me."

"I'm sure she would have left you by then."

"But not for Marc. You wouldn't have allowed that, would you. That's why she killed herself. She found out about you. She knew. She saw it was impossible. She ran out of choices."

She nodded.

"You loved Marc."

"I adored him."

"And your husband knew about it?"

"He only suspected it. Marc was my first affair, it was the first time I was unfaithful."

"And do you still adore him?"

"It's over," she said. "It's all finished."

"Why should I believe that?"

"It's over because of you, because you and I are a couple now."

My mind filled with fragments of ideas, tiny half-glimpsed insights. "You remember that first day you saw me?"

"In the restaurant."

"I was with Marc. And you knew I'd be there."

She lowered her eyes. "Look, we've got to get going."

"Not yet. Wait. You went there on purpose, didn't you. You went to the restaurant because Marc told you he'd be there, you wanted to see him. You and he arranged it." It dawned on me: "And you brought your husband along, you made him take you there for a reason. You would have done anything to keep Marc. What was it, Denise?"

She seemed distracted, she looked at her watch, she shrugged. "I don't remember, it doesn't matter now."

I thought of the woman I had seen him with earlier, coming out of a hotel, walking to a bar. Not Denise, not Kate, but a kind of reflection of them.

"And you must have read Marc's novel?"

She nodded and smiled. "Oh yes."

"Why couldn't Kate translate it?"

She said: "It wasn't supposed to happen this way, you know. It wasn't. If only you'd left it alone. If you had only accepted your wife's death for what it was."

"But I had to know."

"But that wasn't the beginning of the story, it didn't start there."

I still couldn't see it, not all of it. Or rather I must have known it and yet couldn't completely take it in, I had to be content with bits and pieces, a corner, a glimpse. "You told him, didn't you. You knew my name and you told your husband you were having an affair with me. You let it out so he would leave you and Marc alone."

And her silence confirmed it.

"Then what the hell is this all about? It can't be love, not this, not what we're going to do tonight."

She opened the door and stepped out into the deserted half-lit corridor. We waited for the elevator. "And what if I refuse to go through with this?" I said. "If Marc is alive I don't have to do this, do I, there's no need to go through with it."

"Then you don't get *me*, David."

I followed her through the lobby and out into the street. It had begun to snow and the city streets, the shop windows decorated for the holiday, glowed and sparkled in the night. Beneath the merriment of the season was a layer of darkness. I waited with her until she could find a taxi. In the light from the street lamp I could see her staring me in the eye, trying to convince me of the truth of her words. Tonight there would be an accident not half a mile from there, a man would be struck down in the road. We would meet back at her hotel. We would be free.

Between death and life anything could happen.

Meet me. I must see you.

Today. This afternoon. Tonight.

Now.

And she thinks.

And she thinks.

She lifted her hand in the air as the lights changed and the traffic began to move. The sidewalk was crowded with Christmas shoppers, people hurrying to restaurants and shows. She strained to hail a cab, stretching her arm above her head. I went on walking until I disappeared from view.

30

I SPY

Open your eyes.

How much does the artist see?

Only the shapes of things, the way the light falls upon them, the luminous gradations of late afternoon on a woman's jacket? Is his world merely a series of contours and spatial relationships and colors?

Like a novelist does he imagine the plots, the indiscretions, the things that take place behind his back and might never, in a lifetime, come to light?

Does he see into the hearts of others? Or only into his own heart, which bears the reflections of those in his life?

What do you know, as you sit there, book in hand?

Where is she at this moment?

What's he up to, now that he's out of your sight?

Where do the whispers come from?

The artist has added one and one and come up with two. He

knows the man in the red jacket, he's seen him in action, they've spent time together: in taverns drinking gin, smoking pipes, staring at the fire. He's imagined him exchanging looks with his wife; sending notes; making himself at home in her bedroom. In a sense he has created the man in red, a potential trespasser on his marriage: an impending drama. And creation implies destruction. Catastrophe, breakdown, crash, crisis, death, doom, failure, finish, ruin. Calamity, cataclysm, debacle, misfortune, tragedy. Not to mention heartbreak. The very stuff of art.

All he has to do is shut his eyes and the man disappears: a trace of red on a tiled floor; a jacket floating in the canal. The silence of revenge. His art aspires to the elusive stillness of the present, the fugitive moment.

How much can the artist do? Is he capable of murder, of altering the events of the lives of others? Or can he only sit back and create the puzzle for us to fit together? *Hss,* says his brush as he fills in the details, the feather in the man's hat, the stripe on the sleeve, a glimmer of gold between his fingers. Heads or tails?

How much does he want to know when he paints:

a woman holding a balance;

a woman tying on a strand of pearls;

a woman reading a letter?

Perhaps all he's trying to capture is the mystery of these moments, and maybe this is the true essence of art. We are left to invent our own stories, each contradicting the other. He sent the letter; she sent the letter: two different roads leading to the same dead end, the same ambiguous poses we've seen a thousand times.

A late afternoon in Delft. We can almost see him, can't we, sitting in his chair in his studio, looking from one canvas to another, a woman weighing pearls and gold, a woman reading a letter, a woman dreaming at a table: seeking the thread of narrative, the story that will link these individual moments into one grand plot.

Plot, counterplot.

He has missed the point. The woman looks away from him and smiles to herself as the scales come into balance. Everyone in Delft is an artist.

Bzz, say the flies.

31

BALANCING ACT

She began in the upper-left corner.

She wore faded jeans and a white shirt rolled to the elbows. I watched her from a distance, from the other side of the studio, I still hadn't seen her face. I watched as from the white rectangle she began to disclose a world that grew more definite, shapes and strokes reflecting one another. She stood back for a moment, cocked her head. Then she painted over what she had done and began again.

"Remember that you're digging into things other than what you're seeing," Professor Martin was saying. It was the way he started all his lectures: I'd heard it a hundred times before, his voice booming through the hallways of the college.

He avoided my eye as he walked from one student to another, gesturing at their canvases, moving his hand through the air, occasionally smoothing down his short, greying beard: I was an intruder, a man who worked with words, who never soiled his hands in the practice of his art; somehow related to the critics

who with a few well-chosen sentences can destroy a career, an-
nihilate the mystery of things.

The light in the studio was unbroken: it came from strips of
fluorescent bulbs that cast an even, uninspiring glow on the easels
below. The platform was deserted. Often someone would be standing there, naked, pale, shivering, hand on hip, head turned away.
Or there would be a display of some sort, a clutter of objects,
vases, a bowl of fruit on a crumpled rug. Now it was empty, unlit.
The fifteen students there could look only within themselves.

I had finished meeting with my first classes of the semester, the
students staring glassily at me as I spoke of the work expected of
them, the nightly readings, the essays they were required to write
each week. "Any questions?" I asked, and they shook their heads
before silently filing out of the classroom, half of them leaving
their mimeographed syllabuses on their desks.

" 'What the hell are you doing in my parlor?' said the spider
to the fly," Martin bellowed as he came around to the back of the
studio where I sat by the windows. "You don't see me loitering
around during your lectures, do you?"

"I just wanted to observe."

He laughed and slapped me on the shoulder. "Put me in your
next book, why don't you." He spoke like a retired sea captain,
his accent coastal and briny, his language coarse and direct. This
was no academician. Stroking his beard, pulling on a cigarette,
demonstrating technique, his hands were small and powerful, his
fingers thick and knobby: the hands of a painter, hands accustomed
to remaining steady for hours on end. His work was elemental, it
gave off smells of gesso and acrylics and oils and turpentine; physical
work, where your body was engaged in the service of your art.
Not the quiet refinement of what I did: the sentences and paragraphs appearing on a white sheet of paper, the hours of sitting,
the long periods of reflection and debate.

"Back to the grind then, eh?"

I smiled. "Finally."

"Writing again?"

"Soon. I hope. Very soon." I had two choices: I could sacrifice everything to my writing, reinventing my life from one book to the next; or I could make art an extension of my life, one reflecting the other.

I looked across the room again where the woman had resumed painting, her back to me. Her blond hair caught my eye. Shoulder-length and thick.

He laughed and slapped me on the back. "You horny bastard."

And I laughed.

I felt on the verge of imagination: soon I would begin to write again, I would begin to put words together, I would give life to my characters, I would once again step back and glory in the mystery of things. "Go on, look around, look if you have to," he said, lighting another cigarette. "Jesus," I heard him muttering and laughing to himself. "Everyone's a goddamn artist."

I walked across the room and stood behind the woman I'd been watching. Against the white background there was now a square, something resembling a frame. She chose a narrower brush and began adding sharpness and detail to it. Still she hadn't turned to me. Perhaps she didn't know I was there, directly behind her, watching her, watching the canvas. The fluorescent light cast a sickly artificial luster over the studio. I thought of the light in Vermeer's paintings, how well defined it was, how it seemed to seek out the person in the room, the woman reading a letter, putting on her necklace, weighing pearls and gold. Here it was diffuse, unfocused.

Within the frame she'd painted she began to add yet another square, slightly skewed, an echo of the first.

"Do you mind my watching?"

She shook her head.

"Does it matter if I ask questions?"

"Yes."

"Then I'll keep my mouth shut."

I realized how quiet the studio had become. No one but the professor was speaking. Fifteen brushes worked at once, whispering as they made contact with the canvas. In half an hour I would drive slowly home along the icy roads, past the schools and riding academies, the shuttered farm stands. The house would be silent: now there was only me. The last I had seen of Denise Casterman was that Saturday night in the city, waiting for a taxi. Perhaps she was there still, in some perpetual present tense, waiting to move forward in time, to see how her life would proceed.

I didn't bother driving to see her husband; I didn't need to, for if I shut my eyes I could clearly imagine him standing on the corner, waiting in the cold for his wife. I had spared him his end, brutal and metallic. As though trapped within the last scene of a novel he was still there, leaning against a lamppost, lighting a cigarette. Periodically he checks his watch, mumbles under his breath. The rubbish of the day, shreds of paper and empty tin cans, sweeps down the wide potholed avenue, dusty squalls carry grit to his eye. Overhead a plane circles the city, waiting for permission to land, the lighted windows framing other lives, murderous thoughts and high hopes, business appointments and baleful reunions.

The first snowflakes begin to fall. No one comes.

The reader shuts the book, mulls over what might have happened next.

I was left only with my speculations. When I got back to Massachusetts I thought of ringing up all the major banks in Boston. Just to see. Just to know. Simply to find out. Bizarre notions came to mind, I pictured one person after another, following, following. Kate walking to the subway station that morning, Denise behind her. And behind her the judge, watching, waiting. Whose plot was it: Denise's, her husband's, Marc's, one trying to free himself from the others? I had been drawn into a fiction, a machine designed by Denise for one purpose: to extricate herself from the net. Had she felt anything at all for me? Could I look back on these events and find evidence for a burgeoning love? Or would I see it simply because I wanted to?

Now I wanted to make contact with her, listen to her voice, enjoy the luxury of quietly hanging up, breaking the connection. As though I hadn't already destroyed it. In the end I preferred the silence, the doubt, eventually the ignorance. There were a hundred different answers, a multitude of plots that could be woven around these people: Marc, Kate, the judge. I imagine Denise with Marc at this very moment, in a hotel room perhaps, in bed, plotting against her husband. Whom would she find this time to do the deed? There was no end to it.

I imagined her, but not the details, the shabby little pictures like those I had of my wife and her lover climbing the stairs, struggling on the bed for their momentary pleasure. The words exchanged afterwards, the breathless, terse pillow talk. *I love it when you do that. Yes oh yes.*

No. I learned that my wife had been too complex for me to possess her. I should have accepted Kate's death for the mystery it was, a private act, a moment demanding no speculation, no footnotes or afterwords; a striving for serenity, a desire for an end. The artistry of last things. Perhaps that was why Vermeer's paintings are of people caught in the midst of life, captured like a still from a film, a photograph; each a moment from a long intrigue, each suggesting a richer life, a life of contradictions. Perhaps that was why she had given them to me.

There she is, at the table that first time, businesslike, indifferent to me. *Of course I'd prefer to be translating books,* I could hear her saying. *I'm going to continue to ignore your comments, by the way.*

At Covent Garden Market. That lovely rich laugh as she touched my arm.

Lying in bed with me in the heat of love, her hands in my hair.

Walking outside our house amidst the webs, withdrawn, utterly alone.

The Kate who had professed her love for Marc, who had told him she loved him, who had thrown herself at him, was not the Kate I knew.

I had married a woman who remained a stranger to me. But it didn't matter; not really. Perhaps the great failing of even the most aloof of artists is that, though they apply a critical eye to a page of print or a detail on a canvas, they fall blindly in love; and fall hard. They see nothing but what they wish to see.

Frames within frames. I watched the muscles in her arm become taut as she carefully added another line, broad and brown, the rich red brown of a mahogany.

I asked where the light came from.

She said nothing; I was forbidden to talk to her.

"I must know."

Without turning she said quietly, "What do you mean?"

"You know," I said. "Where do you get the light, how do you put it in your painting?"

Then she said: "The light?" She stopped painting, the tip of her brush an inch away from the canvas. "You have to discover it for yourself." And she turned and smiled at me, she laughed and shook her head and then stopped laughing and looked at me, directly at my eyes, and I think I knew then that I would never let her go.

Some things in life are irresistible.

IN THE PICTURE

The artist thinks continually of death.

He thinks of his own death and he thinks of his wife's death, he imagines the house in Delft without her, he shuts his eyes and she's gone. He opens them and she's standing there, holding the scales in her right hand, her eyes lowered, seemingly unaware of him. Life and death in the blink of an eye.

Now listen. Imagine the house devoid of whispers, the noise of a chair scraping across the kitchen floor, the broom as it goes *hss, hss*. He puts his hands over his ears and hears only the sound of the blood coursing through his body.

What does the artist imagine when he thinks of the future: the darkness of the grave, the appalling hollow feeling of eternity? Does he foresee the objects that fly, the pictures that move on a screen, the cars that will one day park outside his house, discharge passengers, fill with shopping bags, hold lovers as they whisper in a line of traffic along the canals? Does he envisage a man at his desk, writing these words? Or can he think only of other artists, sitting on creaking chairs in their studios, capturing the present because the future cannot bear thinking about?

He will never know what posterity will make of him, and perhaps while he paints he doesn't care, for he lives in the moment of each canvas; his presence implied by the painting's existence. He might be utterly forgotten, or simply a line of fine print in the history of art. *Once upon a time there was a painter named Vermeer; now unknown.*

And if his paintings are forgotten, lost in the clutter of history, does that mean the end of Catharina and himself, the end of memory?

Think of it.

An empty house.

The lingering odor of paint.

The dust of a thousand afternoons.

An angle of sunlight poised in a lifeless room.

There's one more painting in which she appears. A curtain has been pulled aside to let us look for ourselves. She's standing in her husband's studio, before a map of the United Netherlands. When we see the room we are reminded of its ghosts: women reading letters, weighing gold and pearls, smiling into mirrors. On the table in front of her lie various objects and clothes, among them a large gilt mask, its eyes aimed at the ceiling. What has it witnessed, this face: the fall of families, the murder of princes, bloodstains on the floor after a night of vengeance? And what has it heard? The murmur of love, the clipped spiteful words? Or is it as blind and deaf as it seems to be: just a mask; something for concealing the truth?

Opposite her, wearing that black hat again and the silly costume he put on to visit the procuress with the man in the red jacket, when like Judas he had turned to confront the betrayed one, the artist sits at his easel, his back to us, indifferent to our existence. Indifferent, yes, but also aware of us, for an audience is implied by the very nature of the scene. That curtain, pulled aside to give us a better look. As though a magician in the midst of an illusion were saying, *Watch carefully. Here's how it's done.*

But who is holding it for us?

The artist's right hand is steadied by a maulstick. He's in the process of painting the laurel leaves that grace her head. For an instant, though, he's stopped, he's turned to look at her.

It's their big moment.

See how she's dressed, look at her props. She wears the blue robes of another time, some mythical epoch; certainly she couldn't go out for a stroll along the canal garbed like that. Too chilly: she would catch her death of cold. The crown of laurel on her head signifies Fame. Though her face is turned towards the artist, though she seems to be smiling, her eyes are downcast, her expression impossible to read. She holds a huge book in her left hand, pressing it to her bosom. In her right hand she grasps a trumpet.

Too heavy.

Shh. Stand still.

In a moment she'll drop them both and the picture will collapse in the shared laughter of artist and model.

She's meant to be Clio, Muse of history. The history of the world, of the Netherlands. Of Catharina Bolnes, of her husband Johannes Vermeer; of both of them together.

Memory: time past, time passing, captured in a single moment, in hundreds and millions of them by all the artists who have ever lived. The artist need not show his face, it's his work that matters. One day, perhaps, he will be famous.

Only Catharina's face can be seen: because of her, because of his genius at recreating her, together they will outlive themselves. They have each other, that's all: here in this studio, artist and model, artist and artist. This *is* the world. He does not even anticipate the millions of people who will stand before his thirty-five paintings wondering what is going through the woman's mind as she reads the letter, sleeps at her table, makes lace. Prognostication is beyond his capacity.

But now there can be no pretense, no manipulation of reality: she's obviously modeling for him. She's not always been happy in this role: playing second fiddle to his talent, his reputation. Always being watched by him: in the morning as she wakes, the sunlight falling across her face; in the late afternoon when light encloses her in a silken mist. But they have eleven children to support, and models brought in from neighboring houses cost many a guilder. Yet it's her face we will never forget: her expression as she puts on her strand of pearls, reads a letter, weighs things.

Look at the light, see how it falls upon her.

It can only be late afternoon.

I looked up from my desk, from the words I had just typed. She had finished painting for the day, cleaned her brushes, changed her shirt. She turned the easel to the wall so that tomorrow she would see it fresh, note where changes had to be made; whether it had to be done over, or replaced by another image. Now she was reading her mail, standing by the window in the bedroom, her knuckles white with the sheet of paper between them, her face betraying four different emotions. Fear. Anger. Relief. Joy.

Frames within frames.

David went back to work. He thought of an evening she might leave him and a morning, far in the future, when she would die, and somehow between them and around them there was a story to be told. None of us deserves the banality of real life. For us there is only the richness of art.

Oh yes. There's one last thing: the painting of the artist in his studio hangs in a museum in Vienna.

Vienna.

And she turned her face to look. But she didn't see me.